LOST MOTHER . . .
LOST CHILD . . .

"It's no longer your case, I'm assigning it to some-one else."

Cletus said, "If you do that, I'll find the mother herself, and see that every newspaper in the country prints the story of how you let four years go by without making an effort to locate the mother and see if she was now able to care for her child."

The look Mrs. Bok gave him traveled on a direct beam of pure hate. She was too angry to speak. Her lips were tight together and her hands were doubled into fists.

"There is one little fact," Cletus continued, "that will make you look bad when Mary Kalinski sues you for a million dollars. And that is the fact that she wouldn't have been hard to find. You know why?"

There was no change in the expression on Mrs. Bok's face.

"All you had to do was to check the telephone book. It's right here, Mary Kalinski. Right here in Farmington." And he walked out.

WHY WOULD I LIE?

FORMERLY TITLED "THE FABRICATOR" BY
HOLLIS HODGES

◆ AVON
PUBLISHERS OF BARD, CAMELOT AND DISCUS BOOKS

This work was previously published under the title
THE FABRICATOR.

AVON BOOKS
A division of
The Hearst Corporation
959 Eighth Avenue
New York, New York 10019

Copyright © 1976 by Hollis Hodges
Published by arrangement with Crown Publishers, Inc.
Library of Congress Catalog Card Number: 75-40314
ISBN: 0-380-01918-3

First Avon Printing, March, 1978
Second Printing

AVON TRADEMARK REG. U.S. PAT. OFF. AND IN
OTHER COUNTRIES, MARCA REGISTRADA,
HECHO EN U.S.A.

Printed in the U.S.A.

to Candy

*One fascinating
thing about sports
is that after every game
you can always
look back and see
just where was the
turning point.*

CURT GOWDY

Chapter 1

Cletus Hayworth was the grandson, on his father's side, of a noted theologian and convicted rapist. At twenty-five years of age he had so far shown no tendency in either direction.

Cletus was tall, slender, serious-looking, with black hair that curled down over his ears and onto his shirt collar. He had brown eyes and a dark mustache that curled down at the ends. To his neighbors in the apartment building he was seen as a quiet, well-behaved, polite young man who brought girls home occasionally for overnight. Those who saw him playing in the park with Hank on Sunday morning presumed him to be a loving father. To his co-workers he was a man of good humor, not too easy to understand or get close to, and mildly eccentric. He smoked cigarettes and occasionally a pipe. He was moderate in his smoking, as he was in most things. His vices were few and mainly of the forgivable kind. In general, people liked him. Some envied him. A few emulated him. None hated him. Quite a large number would say without hesitation that you couldn't believe a damn thing he said.

Cletus Hayworth was the originator and sole practitioner of the form of mental therapy known as fabrication.

Cletus defined a fabrication as a seemingly plausible story or statement told as if it were true, which it could be, but which in fact it happened not to be. But moreover—and most important—it would be of no particular significance even if it *were* true.

In his more optimistic moments Cletus viewed the practice of fabrication as the inevitable replacement for the outdated theories of Freud. People everywhere would find it easy to get their heads together and sanity would sweep the country. Politicians would become honest and love would prevail. However, in his more troubled moments he groaned a lot, often awakening at four o'clock in the morning, wondering how to get himself and his best friend out of the trouble fabrication had got them into.

One of the few people to whom he gave even a partial explanation of fabrication was Hank. And Hank, extremely bright young lad though he was, did not really understand the fundamentals underlying the theory. This was not a fair test, however, as Hank was only six years old.

The night the subject was discussed the boy was in bed, after prayers, and Cletus was standing by the bureau near the door, smoking his pipe.

"That last part," Cletus said, "is essential. That it would be of no significance even if it *were* true. Otherwise it simply becomes a lie. And I don't want you to go around telling lies. Right?"

Hank said, "Right."

Cletus said, "The definition I gave you is probably not the one in the dictionary. It's mine." He took a moment to light his pipe.

He said, "A fabrication is different from a lie. A lie is a deliberate untruth regarding a matter of some importance and told for the purpose of deceiving. And that, too, is only my definition."

He said, "Nor is it the same as a gross exaggeration, which is a distortion of something presented as fact. And a fact, as we all know, is something that is true."

Hank's young brow furrowed as he strained to follow this difficult line of thought.

Cletus continued. "Facts, Hank, are the very foundation of human society. Without facts we would all be lost. Facts have forever been the basis of our understanding of the world we live in."

He lit his pipe once more. Then went on. "History," he said, "is resplendent with beautiful facts. For instance, it was once a fact that the earth was flat. And that the sun revolved around the earth once a day. Rain or shine."

He gave the lad time to absorb that information.

"Now it's round. Pretty much.

"But that's heavy stuff. Don't worry your young head about it."

Not only was Hank just six years old, but he had been six only four days.

The subject of fabrication had arisen because Hank had accused Cletus of telling Mrs. Gogle, the baby-sitter, a lie when he told her on the telephone that she wouldn't have to do the dishes tonight because he'd already done them for a change. He hadn't done them at all. He and Hank had gone to Burger Heaven for hamburgers and there simply had not been any dishes to do. But Mrs. Gogle always said, when he called, leave the dishes and I'll take care of them for you.

Hank had said, "You lied to Mrs. Gogle," and his face had showed real concern. He had been taught that people who told lies went to hell. And he didn't want that to happen to his favorite person in the whole world.

Hank was a handsome, intelligent, healthy boy with blond hair and bright blue eyes. He sat in bed, relaxed, leaning back, a smile waiting just beneath the surface, ready to break through. He was happy. This was his favorite time of day, between prayers and lights out, when they rapped, as Cletus called it, about things. Some nights when Cletus got talking about funny things Hank would get laughing so hard he'd have trouble getting to

11

sleep. Sometimes he'd wake up in the middle of the night laughing.

Cletus had explained that he had simply got tired of hearing Mrs. Gogle try to show how good she was by always offering to do the dishes. The truth was that whether there were no dishes because he'd done them, or because they'd gone out to eat, could not possibly be of any significance whatsoever to the baby-sitter. And that had led to his explaining the difference between a lie and a fabrication.

"Now that we have disposed of that matter," Cletus said, "I have a few comments to make about your prayers."

The boy rolled his eyes toward the ceiling in mock impatience. His prayers. Not that again!

"In general," Cletus said, "I continue to note improvement. Your prayers have become more bearable during the last few weeks. No more of that long dull list of all the people you've ever known. Bless this person. Bless that person."

He said, "Lord, I thought I'd fall asleep listening to you go down the list."

Cletus shifted position. "And that bit about bless my good father and my mother, wherever she is. I got a couple things to say about that."

Hank sighed deeply once more. It was so difficult having a father!

"I took you out for hamburgers, and I told you I'd take you out again tomorrow night. So you don't have to give me that 'Bless my good father' routine."

Hank put a hand across his face to try to hide the smile.

"As for the 'mother, wherever she is' bit, that's corny. Your mother knows where she is. You make it sound like she's lost, or something. Lost in the jungle. Without food or water."

He looked solemnly at the boy for a moment. "And

you're always wanting everybody to be blessed. Why don't you ever suggest He smite somebody?"

Hank didn't know what that meant, but he knew it was something funny so he laughed.

The boy had a good laugh. Light and free. A happy thing to hear.

Cletus moved over and kissed him, quickly. Almost brusquely. As if the boy were getting too big for that kind of thing.

"Now good night." And he started toward the door.

But Hank wasn't quite ready to end this part of his day. He called after him, "You going out?"

Cletus said, "Of course I'm going out. Why do you think I called Mrs. Gogle?" He flipped the light switch and the room went dark.

Hank said, "Oh. You going to wear your helmet?"

"No."

Hank had time for one last question. "You going to bring anyone home with you?"

He liked it when Cletus brought a girl home. Breakfast was more fun. The girl always laughed a lot and Cletus did too. And usually there was something special, like pancakes and sausages.

Cletus half turned and laughed. "I will if I can. The girl who was here last time."

Kay. That was good. Hank had liked her.

"So go to sleep. You should have been asleep ten minutes ago."

Hank said, "Good night."

Cletus called back, "Good night."

He got a can of beer from the refrigerator and stood by the window looking down the narrow street between the long rows of attractive apartments that constituted Fairlawn Estates. It was August. Well-dressed adults strolled casually or stood chatting beside the gaslight lampposts. Occasionally a young couple would come out of one of the apartments and walk toward the parking lots, he usually in a tie and coat, she maybe even wearing a corsage. This was that kind of place. He had been here six weeks and he still found the scene as disquieting and alien to his personality as ever.

Where he used to live, on Fourth Street, from the window you could see the lights of Sandy's Bar and Grill and if the wind was right you could hear the jukebox. And probably no girl had walked down that street wearing a corsage since Sandy's youngest daughter was married two years ago.

Fairlawn Estates was on the southern edge of Farmington. Looking north, you could see the lights of the city. Population, fifty-nine thousand, about eight thousand of whom worked for the New England Manufacturing Company. That and the state college kept the town alive. And it wasn't very much alive at that.

Twenty-two miles to the east was Cranesville, where he had been born. He didn't go there much anymore. When he did, he wore the helmet.

For maybe as long as five minutes he stood there, thinking about his home town, his family, his childhood. A girl named Heidi Zimmerman and a young cop named Devanny. The helmet. Hank.

He went into his bedroom and got the helmet off the bureau. It was an old miner's helmet, maroon colored, laminated plastic over cloth. Shaped like a construction worker's hat except that it was higher and not as long. And it had a metal piece in front where the lamp would fit into. Inside, under the rear rim, was

M.S.A. SKULLGARD
TYPE K
MINE SAFETY APPLIANCES CO.
PITTSBURGH, PA.   MADE IN U.S.A.

He'd bought it the afternoon that the newspaper headlines told that Devanny had died. That was a little more than four years ago.

He didn't wear the helmet as much as he used to. He still wore it when he visited his family in Cranesville. And to Dr. Barber's office. But he didn't wear it to work much anymore. Occasionally when it was raining or snowing. Or when he had something heavy on his mind. Like the Mary Kalinski case that he'd been involved with for the last six weeks.

Mary Kalinski! He put the helmet on.

He finished the beer, tossed the can into the waste-basket, and walked into Hank's bedroom again. He called softly, "Hank, you awake?"

No answer. So a little louder. "You 'wake?" But still silence.

He leaned against the doorframe, relaxed, eyes on the boy's blond head on the pillow. He took a cigarette from the pack but didn't light it. Just clutched it in his fist like a stick or club. He said, "Sorry you're not awake, because I had another thought or two about your prayers."

He took a few moments to adjust his eyes to the semi-darkness. It was a small bedroom designed for young children. Pink and blue flowered wallpaper with scattered figures from storybook fame. Jack and Jill. Little Miss Muffet. Peter Rabbit. That kind of thing. The effect in this particular bedroom had been softened by a large print of Picasso's *Guernica* at one end of the room and a poster of Jane Fonda at the other. There was an antiwar poster over the boy's bed.

Cletus said, "I wanted to talk to you about that part toward the end when you stop praying out loud and go into executive session for about ten seconds."

He explained, "That means secret session. No outsiders. I often wonder what you're saying during that period."

There was no response from the boy. The room was quiet. Cletus waited another moment, then said, "You probably wouldn't tell me, even if you were awake."

A longer silence. "I hope it's not that you're asking if it
15

could be arranged for your old man to go back to where he came from so you could return to the life you were leading before I came back upon the scene."

A longer silence this time. Quite a while.

"I would understand, of course. Life was more secure for you those days, I guess."

He put the cigarette to his lips and lit it.

Then, in a low, serious tone, he said, "One thing you can be sure of, if you're asking to get away from me it's going to be a pretty tough thing to do. Because I plan to make you stay with me for a long, long time. Until that far-off day when you're old enough to pack your sleeping bag, throw your guitar over your shoulder, and say that you suppose maybe it's time to be moving along. And that'll be another dozen years, at least."

He smoked silently for a moment. Then, "Even after you go on your own I rather expect that I'll be hearing from you from time to time. Phone calls, if nothing else. Collect, probably."

Then, abruptly, "But enough of this kind of talk," and he left the room. "I'll discuss it with you sometime when you're awake."

Mrs. Gogle rang the doorbell just as he left the bedroom, so he walked over and let her in.

She was a stocky, plain woman in her early fifties. Friendly, gossipy, bighearted. Married, children grown. Her husband was manager of the meat department of the A & P store in town. Worked nights a lot.

He had the helmet in his hand and she, of course, asked about it. She thought it a lovely color.

"Belonged to my father," he said. "Pennsylvania coal miner. One of the best, they tell me. Died in an accident when I was only four years old. Barely remember him."

Her quick expression of sympathy was followed by puzzlement. Hadn't he said his family had come from New York City? A policeman? Killed in the line of duty?

16

"That was my stepfather," Cletus said. "Mother married a second time."

She said, "Well! Can you imagine that? I'd have sworn you said you were born in Greenwich Village."

"No," he said, "I mentioned that I had *lived* in Greenwich Village."

It still bothered her. She remembered so distinctly. Cletus said, "I wouldn't lie to you, would I?" and she replied very indignantly, "Of course not!"

What did he think she was that she would think he would lie to her.

She carried a thin pink sweater, which she now tossed on the sofa. "Boy asleep?"

He said, "Yes. Sound asleep."

She said, "That's good. He goes to sleep so nice."

Before leaving, Cletus returned to his bedroom and tossed the helmet onto the bureau. Mrs. Gogle headed for Hank's room. "I'll just check him out. Make sure he's tucked in."

She always did that. It was part of the ritual of the changing of the guard.

Cletus had the front door open by the time she reappeared. It gave her great amusement to inform him, with a hearty laugh, that once again, like the last two times she'd been here, he had been wrong about the boy.

"Nope," she said, "he wasn't really asleep. Just fooling you again."

She added, "He said to tell you good night."

Before he closed the door behind him, Cletus called out, "Good night, Hank."

Chapter 2

Perhaps the turning point for Cletus was the afternoon
Pamela Treybold picked him up in her fire red Jaguar
and took him home with her.

That had been two years ago. He was twenty-three.
She was maybe a year older. Brunette, a good sense of
humor, a sensuous figure that stopped just short of being
chubby but at nothing else. She had money, an apartment in the Roseboro section, and a compulsive need to
sleep with married men. Her psychiatrist had traced this
compulsion to the experience of having entered unan-
nounced her parents' bedroom at age thirteen and having seen her father, whom she loved dearly, making love
to her mother. In that instant—more than an instant, actually, for she had watched until the act had reached its
normal conclusion—there had been implanted in her
mind the desire to make love to married men, all of
whom would symbolically represent her father. She
would come between every man and his wife, break up
every marriage. She would show who was really the most
loved.

The psychiatrist who first treated her for this mental
aberration is still paying alimony to a wife in Larchmont,
New York.

(Never prior to that fateful afternoon had his wife happened to have a camera with her.)

Cletus first met her the day he was interviewed and
hired by Dr. Morton Thruston, headmaster of Marleboro
Mountain, a private coed prep school in Atherton, six

miles west of Farmington. Dr. Thruston had introduced her to Cletus as the teacher he would be replacing in September. Miss Treybold had taught social studies and intermediate English. She would not be returning in the fall. Nor would the school's athletic instructor, who had been caught with her in a most compromising position on the couch in his office by two young girls seeking fresh shuttlecocks for their badminton game. Remaining at the school, but under probation, were a fifty-four-year-old Latin teacher, a once happily married thirty-one-year-old instructor in American history, plus the grounds-keeper, Mr. Barnes, and the head cook, Coakley, father of four.

They had met again, a month later, on a Saturday afternoon in June. She was waiting at a stoplight in downtown Farmington when he walked by. They waved. She offered him a ride.

It amused her to learn that he was on his way to the library. She said, "Don't take your new job too seriously. You won't need to spend the summer preparing your lessons. The kids at Marleboro cut most classes anyway."

For a few moments there was between them the feeling that comes when two people are together who both recognize they don't like the other one very much. He was not her type. Nor she his. He had accepted the ride only out of politeness. The same reason that she had offered it.

She asked, "What are you going to be studying at the library?" Adding, "It's too nice a day, really, for anyone to spend it indoors studying anything."

What he had been planning to study was a young woman he had met two nights ago at a party who had said she worked there.

He said, "Just studying."

"Something important, I suppose."

He thought a moment. "Not terribly important, I suppose. But rather nice." And he hoped that would end the conversation.

"What kind of project? Elizabethan poetry?" And she laughed.

It was none of her business who or what he was going to study. And whether or not she approved was of no interest to him. He tried to think of something suitably absurd.

He came up with, "Movie stars." And nodded his head. He liked that. "I'm studying movie stars."

She laughed so hard she almost ran into the car ahead that had stopped for a red light.

She said, "Why, for God's sake, are you interested in movie stars?"

He said, "It's a long story." Implying that it was not worth the long time it would take to tell it. But she had to know. She'd die of curiosity if he didn't tell her.

He paused so long before answering that she had to ask again why he was interested in movie stars. He finally said, "My wife. It's because of her."

She looked at him with increased interest. "I didn't know you were married."

He said that he was, and happily. "Except that my wife is in love with Rock Hudson."

The light turned green. The car behind them honked.

"It's not just my wife," he said. "It's her mother, too. The two of them spend all day looking through movie magazines. It's all they talk about."

She said, "God! How awful." And, "What's your wife like?"

He said, "Like her mother. *Exactly* like her mother. They wear the same clothes, same hairstyle." He gestured with his hands above and around his head to indicate a kind of bouffant style.

He said, "This morning I walked from the bright sunlight outdoors into the house and for a few moments I couldn't tell which was which."

She said, "That's awful."

He said, "Then one of them giggled and I swear that

20

for a moment I couldn't tell if it had come from my wife or my mother-in-law."

"Lord," she said, "that's hard to believe."

He asked, "Would I lie to you?" and she said, "I suppose not."

They went almost a half block in silence.

"What I'm going to do," Cletus said, "is read up on movie stars. Maybe I'll find that Rock Hudson is queer, or something. Or has syphilis or hemorrhoids." He said it was the only way he could save his marriage. "The truth is that I still love her, regardless."

At this point they reached the library. But she didn't stop. She didn't even slow down. She said, "You poor son of a bitch! You don't need the library. What you need is a good stiff drink." And she drove him to her place.

They lay in bed, pleasantly relaxed, the late afternoon sun through the partially closed window shades giving a rosy glow to their naked bodies. They sipped Scotch and talked. She had the most beautifully constructed body he had ever been next to, and as he talked, his hands moved along the perfect lines, cupped the abundant breasts, smoothed the already smooth thighs and rounded hips.

His appreciation of the beauty of her body interested her less than the story of his marriage, so they were back on that subject.

She asked, "Then, why did you marry her?"

He explained why, but to do so he had to tell her the story of his family, and it was a long story.

He told her that he'd never really known much about his father. How he made a living, that kind of thing. His father had owned the apartment building they lived in and collected rents. Maybe that was his only income. But his father had traveled a lot, so maybe he was a salesman.

"About my father, I remember most one summer afternoon. We had just finished lunch. I was waiting for a friend to come by so we could go swimming."

He let his hands glide across the ripe expanse of stom-

21

ach down to where was the slight swelling with soft pubic hairs. "Father had been slowly pacing up and down, restless, looking at my mother, my older sister, and myself. Thoughtfully. Affectionately. Then he walked over to my sister."

He took a sip of his drink.

"She is two years older than I, my sister. Thin. Shy. Father asked her how things were going and she said fine. He asked her what she was going to do when she grew up and she said she thought she'd clerk in a store like Aunt Margaret, then get married and have a family.

"Father said he thought that was nice, and came over to me. He asked if I had any problems, and I said no. He asked what I thought I'd do when I grew up and I said maybe I'd be a teacher. I was only fourteen at the time, but that's what I said. I still remember that he put his hand on my shoulder, looked me in the eye, and said, 'Good. That's a hard way to learn, my boy, but you can do it.' And we shook hands."

Cletus smiled at the memory. "Incidentally, and strangely enough, my sister did work in a store and then get married and have children. And now I'm going to be a teacher."

He had another sip of Scotch.

"Next he went over to my mother. She was sitting quietly at the table, hands folded in front of her. Head down a bit. Waiting. He went over to her and we heard him say, 'Things seem to be going pretty well, Martha. Quite well. You're well provided for and the children are doing fine.'

"She didn't say anything. Just sat there. Hands folded. And after a moment father said quietly, 'So I think I'll be moving along.'"

Cletus shook the almost empty glass to make the ice cubes bang together. He said, "I remember Mother didn't say anything. Just nodded a time or two. And I remember Father put his hand on top of hers for a moment, then, without looking back, went out the back door and down the back steps, and we heard him get into the old Hudson and drive off."

He added, after a few moments, "That was the last time I saw him."

She pulled him to her and comforted him. "You poor darling."

Later he explained what all that had had to do with his marrying the girl who was indistinguishable from her mother.

"After Father left, my Uncle Charlie, Father's brother, was around the place a lot, helping to fix things, doing errands. Gradually he just sort of moved in and after a year or so, without much being said, he took over Father's place. He was good to my sister and me. It was he who taught me to drive the car, taught me about girls, that kind of thing."

Cletus said, "He was like Father, casual about life and money. Always had some scheme that was going to make him a lot of money. None of the schemes ever worked. The things he and Mother tried got crazier and crazier. My sister finished school and left home. I enrolled in the local college and tried to stay away from the house as much as possible.

"I met this girl, Irma, a simple, rather plain, heavy girl, the kind I ordinarily wouldn't have given much attention to. But she used to invite me to dinner, and any place was better than eating at home and listening to Mother and Uncle Charlie talk about how no doubt there was buried treasure right in the backyard and how they really ought to dig up the whole area sometime."

He said, "Anyway, Irma did things like knit me sweaters, worry about my catching cold, keep after me to do my schoolwork. Let me study at her mother's place. Even then the two were into the movie star thing, but I thought it was only a passing fad. Something they'd lose interest in later on.

"Then one night she'd asked me to take her to a movie

23

and I had to stop by my house to get some money I'd put away in a bureau drawer. I remember we'd gone up the back stairs and entered through the kitchen."

Cletus shook his head at the memory. He laughed softly, then continued. "That was the day after the local paper had reported a story from Enid, Oklahoma, about a man who had bought an old mattress for five bucks and later found thirty thousand dollars hidden in it. So, knowing Mother and Uncle Charlie, I should have known what to expect."

He said, "We walked into the kitchen and there they were. On one side of the kitchen was a stack of old mattresses that Charlie had bought from a junk dealer. And in the middle of the room were Mother and him, up to their knees in cotton mattress stuffing, going through it looking for money."

He said, "I told Irma to stay where she was, and I waded knee-deep through wads of dirty cotton to the bedroom and back, red-faced, disgusted, swearing that I'd leave that house for good.

"I proposed to Irma on the way back down the stairs, and she accepted."

Pamela Treybold wasn't very sympathetic. She said, "That was a dumb thing to do."

He agreed.

"And now you're stuck with a woman you don't like."

Cletus resented her putting it that way. He said it wasn't quite that bad. "She loves me. She's good to me. She does nice things for me. In fact, I still love her."

Pamela laughed lightly and moved her body against his. "You only think you love her."

Later she left him in bed with a fresh drink while she went out to buy some food, wine, and other things. He wanted to go with her, but she insisted he stay at home.

Afterwards, he understood why. She wanted to make a phone call.

24

She brought back a steak, which he broiled while she fixed the salad. They drank the wine, clinking the glasses together, wishing each other future happiness. She in whatever work she did next, he in his new teaching job at Marleboro Mountain. She wished him success working for that old bastard, Dr. Thruston.

She really hated Dr. Thruston. You could tell that. And what made her most angry, she said, was that the old man hadn't been able to keep his eyes off her. Or his hands, either. More than once when she was in his office he suggested that they get together some night so he could help her work out her lesson plans. Some place where it was quiet. And because she had never accepted the suggestion, he had fired her.

After dinner she spread a thick, white, deep pile rug in the middle of the living room floor and said that what she liked to do was lie there naked and watch television and maybe make a little love by the dim glow. And that sounded like fun.

He said that Irma was probably wondering where he was, but he didn't care.

She said, "Forget Irma."

She turned off all the lights and in the soft light of the TV screen they caressed each other, drank wine, and waited for the moment when passion would become so overwhelming that no distraction from the television screen could hold it back another moment.

Many times he thought they'd reached that point, only to have her hold back a little longer. She kept him excited, moved her body about, kissed, teased, stalled. And waited. In the soft light she waited for just the right moment.

And when it came she was ready.

There was a knock on the door. She pulled him upon her, with her legs locked him inescapably into her, and began the movements of love. And called out, "Come in."

Not even the distraction that presented itself in the doorway could keep Cletus from the completion of what he had begun.

Coming into the room, slowly closing the door behind him, trying to adjust his eyes to the dim light, standing there with a happy look of keen anticipation on his face and in his arms a paper bag from which protruded the tops of two bottles of champagne, was Dr. Morton Thruston. And his happy expression gradually gave way to one of bewilderment, disappointment, and hurt.

There, naked, in full view of the director of the school where Cletus had planned to teach the coming school year, engaged in what the old man had himself come here to engage in, Cletus reached that happiest of moments and collapsed in ecstatic and hilarious dismay.

Later that night on his way back to his apartment and his empty bed, Cletus wondered what it would have been like to have had a father who had shaken hands all around and said he thought he would be moving on.

He couldn't picture his own father doing that.

And what would it be like to have a mother who was eccentric? Or to be married to a woman you couldn't tell from your mother-in-law?

In fact, what would it be like to be married to anyone?

Chapter 3

The supervisor of the Division of Children's Services of the Farmington office of the Department of Welfare was Mrs. Adelaide Bok. She had been with the department for twenty-five years. Before that she had been with the Homes for Little Wanderers for four. The kinds of people now coming to the department looking for work sickened her. Long hair, dressed like freaks. Mustaches. Beards. Her husband, who was superintendent of schools in the nearby town of Hathaway, said the same thing. But he didn't have to hire them. Here, when you are short of help and not too many people want to be social workers, sometimes you have to.

The young man sitting across the desk from her was a good example. Hair down to his shirt collar. Dark mustache that curled down at the ends.

She wondered if she could get away with telling him he would have to shave it off. Probably not. But maybe. So she told him, "You'd have to shave off the mustache. We don't encourage them here."

He said he couldn't. "It covers up a scar." And she knew he was lying.

She wondered if he'd had a bath recently.

"You'd look better without it."

He said that without it he looked even worse. "The doctor who sewed up my lip recommended it."

She asked the doctor's name and he named one from the town of Cranesville. She glanced at the application form. Cranesville was the town he had given as his place of birth.

She asked how long he had lived there, and checked his answer against the summary of his background she held in her hand. Sometimes you could catch them lying. If they are liars, it is best to find out right away.

Mrs. Bok was short, stocky, in her middle fifties, had two sons, both married. One with the state police and the other an officer in the Marines. She thought of herself as politically a conservative, and a liberal in human values. She belonged to the Farmington Taxpayers Association but believed that helping the deserving needy was in accordance with the American tradition. Her husband tended to be to the right of her politically.

"We do have an opening," she said, "and at the moment there is no one available from the civil service list. You would have to take the examination when it is given, of course, and pass it."

She studied the application form once more. The educational background was unusual. Two years at Brandeis University, then a one-year gap, then two years at the local state college.

"What were you doing during that year away from school?"

He said that he had traveled, mostly. With seven or eight months in San Francisco.

"We have to check all this," she said. "If there is anything on this application that isn't true, tell me now before we send letters out."

He said it was all true. And she didn't say anything, her silence implying that she temporarily withheld judgment. "This is a difficult job, so I hope you will not take it unless you are willing to work long and hard hours."

He said that he was willing.

"It's not a job for one who isn't serious."

He said that he was serious. "I didn't used to be," he said. "But I am now. I used to be always trying to change

28

things. Protest marches, peace parades. That kind of thing. But now I'm serious."

He added, "And I'll enjoy working with low-income families. I've known that side of life myself."

She said, "You won't be working with low-income families all the time. Our part of the welfare program doesn't deal with aid for dependent children, or general relief, or the aged, or the blind. You would be working with children who have to be placed in foster homes. And most of our foster families are in the middle-income class. Working with them, unfortunately, is often more difficult than working with low-income people."

"I've never been on welfare myself," Cletus admitted. "But I have a sister who was on it for a while. After her husband was killed in a mine cave-in."

Mrs. Bok agreed that it was helpful to have some understanding of the kinds of problems welfare families had.

"And my father died some years ago. So I know about broken homes."

She looked impatient rather than sympathetic. Too many fathers who died left their families unprovided for.

"Both my parents are dead, actually."

"So I see from your application."

A little more for good measure. "I recall my father saying once that he had often wished he'd gone into social work instead of into business."

She didn't respond to that. But she had another comment on the summary. "I notice that you had two years at Brandeis University, then later two years at the state college. That's rather unusual."

He explained that he once thought he wanted to be a teacher. "In fact," he said, "a few months ago I actually accepted a teaching position in a small private school in this area."

She said, "Really? What made you change your mind?"

"I found that the old man who was headmaster of the

29

school was trying to have an affair with one of the young teachers, and it led to a rather awkward scene between us."

She understood his feelings about that, and approved.

"I felt it wasn't the place for me."

She nodded. He had shown good judgment. Then one last observation. "I see you aren't married."

"No."

He went to work the first Monday in July, passed the state exam in October, was given his permanent appointment six months later. He grew to like the job. He even became quite good at it. Mrs. Bok, herself, complimented him on his work.

Once, in a very troublesome case involving a young unmarried mother, she went along with his recommendation, even though she really disagreed with him. He threatened to quit if he didn't get to do what he thought was the right thing to do. And she needed him. In two years he had become better able to manage his case load than anyone else she had ever had working for her. So she agreed to let him handle it his way.

"But if this turns out to be trouble," she said, "I'll personally see that you are fired and never get a job as social worker anywhere again, ever."

He said, "Trust me."

That was the Mary Kalinski case. And it did turn out to be trouble.

Serious trouble.

Chapter 4

It is true that Cletus could honestly say that he was the grandson, on his father's side, of a noted theologian and a convicted rapist. But only if you accept his contention that a person can have two paternal grandfathers.

For the rapist was not a theologian, and most assuredly the theologian was not a rapist.

Cletus's father, born Joe Greiner of Farmington, had been adopted by the Reverend Eldon Hayworth. Cletus reasoned that this made Eldon Hayworth his grandfather. Your father's father is your grandfather.

But he was not willing to disregard his natural grandfather, Herb "Hardtimes" Greiner, unemployed house painter, drunkard, free-lance brawler, and father of five, who once while winding down a three-day drinking spree had awakened to find himself in his small fishing shack by the river in bed with a young girl. Also in the shack was an irate father and two policemen. The latter three had not been invited and had entered without knocking.

Hardtimes Greiner had been fifty years old at the time. The girl a nicely filled-out fourteen.

The five offspring of Hardtimes were Jamie, George, Martha, Joe, and Edna.

Jamie at twenty-two had already spent two six-month terms in the house of correction on breaking and entering charges.

George was on probation for stealing a car and for

nonsupport of his seventeen-year-old wife and infant.

Martha, herself only seventeen, was pregnant, but had no one to demand support payments from.

Joe was fourteen. His little sister, Edna, twelve.

The girl his father had been caught in bed with had been in Joe's class in school. Sometimes, teasingly, she would kiss him when the teacher's back was turned. And laugh because he blushed so red.

He loved her very much. So much that he ran when she came close to him.

The newspaper story of the arraignment of Hardtimes Greiner in district court on the statutory rape charge had included the incidental observation that on the same day Jamie Greiner had been in court and charged with breaking into the poor box at St. Mark's Church.

It was too much.

Joe Greiner, humiliated, angry, almost in tears, left Farmington that day and never set foot in the town again. The last words he had with his mother was to tell her that he was running away, would never return, and not to come looking for him. And she didn't.

Jamie was twice more in the house of correction, had two children by two women, neither of whom he was married to. He wrecked two cars before losing his life and twenty-five dollars in a wager that the ice of Lake Manhassett was still thick enough on the first day of March to bear the weight of himself and his friend's automobile.

So much for Jamie.

George turned out rather well for a Greiner. He supported his wife much of the time, kept out of jail, fathered four boys, all of whom were curly-haired bundles of mischief, likable truants, good football players, and bad insurance risks.

Good for George.

Martha married a young plumber's assistant and in her later years became rather well-to-do. She and her husband owned their own home. Ended up with five more children in addition to the one she already had. Boys all handsome like their father, but not as ambitious. Girls as pretty and vivacious as their mother, but none who married as well.

Too bad for them.

The youngest, Edna, married a soldier and went to Texas. She didn't write home very often the first few years, then not at all.

Joseph, Jr., did quite well for himself. He got as far as Cranesville, a town twenty-two miles away, somewhat smaller than Farmington, was put up for the night by a Reverend Eldon Hayworth. And surely it was God who had directed this strong and willing young man to the home of this childless couple. They welcomed him. Took him into their home and hearts.

Six months later, at the suggestion of the boy himself, they adopted him. He became Joseph Eldon Hayworth. Neither he nor they ever regretted it.

It was at about this time that the Reverend Hayworth made a simple—indeed, obvious—philosophical observation that brought him his small share of fame.

Eldon Hayworth was poor. Very poor. There was no reason to believe that he would ever be otherwise.

His small congregation paid him a very small salary. He could find no other church interested in using his services. He did menial jobs to supplement his income, sometimes doing yard work for the same parishioners who could not afford to pay him a better salary. His wife did housecleaning. They would accept no charity. They had their pride, their religious faith, their righteousness, and their poverty.

The philosophical observation he grasped onto was

33

this: If you find that you are stuck with some condition that is beyond your ability to alter, the only intelligent thing to do is to glorify that particular condition. Which in his case was poverty and the acceptance of it.

The bits of poetry that he sometimes wrote and worked into his Sunday sermons leaped into life.

(Hard life, of course, went with loving wife. Just as sin and divorce went with gin and remorse.)

The Cranesville *Courier* printed his verse. Colonel Hampton, who owned two other newspapers and a large share of the Clayton County Racetrack, felt that these were sentiments that needed wider acceptance. He had himself known what it was like to be poor.

(Poor, of course, rhymed with heaven's door. Just as did pride with far from Jesus' side.)

Reverend Hayworth, with the Colonel's help, arranged for a dozen or more of his best poems to be printed and bound and sent off to the President of the United States. He got back a letter from someone in a government office who thanked him on behalf of the President and assured him that the sentiments so beautifully expressed in the poems would make any American proud of his country.

The letter was printed on the front page of the *Courier*. Attendance at the small church picked up and most parishioners found that by digging a little deeper they could come up with a little something for the collection plate. And for a while at least, in the town of Cranesville, he was a noted theologian.

Joseph Eldon Hayworth hated everything that reminded him of his former life. He could not tolerate the sight of liquor. He detested poor people, lazy people, the criminal, the unfit. He embraced religion, free enterprise, and hard work.

He started as errand boy in a small corner drugstore, worked his way through pharmacy school at the state university, and at the age of thirty-eight owned the store and building.

Four years later he sold both the store and building and bought a bigger one of each.

He married Hope Hester, an orphan and devout Christian, and begat four fine children. Walter, Paul, Faith, and Cletus.

A doctor, lawyer, businesswoman, and Cletus. Just before his untimely death at the age of sixty-two, he was worth five times that of all his brothers and sisters combined.

Ownership of a thriving drugstore and valuable office building had not been enough. With some finanical assistance from a Dr. Creighton, he started a nursing home, which was filled with elderly citizens almost before the lawn was seeded and the flagpole erected in front. The investment was a spectacular success. Other doctors began making discreet inquiries as to how he had started the project and did he need additional financial help in order to start another. Every Wednesday afternoon brought reports from his staff of a crowd of well-dressed professional people just sort of looking around.

And an idea was implanted.

Sunset Nursing Homes, Inc., was born. On his own, this time, borrowing heavily from the local bank, he set up a corporation that franchised nursing homes the way Burger Heaven franchised hamburger stands. For an amount of money that any two or three doctors could raise without difficulty, the corporation would oversee the erection of a suitable building, provide full operating plans and procedures, give instructions in the hiring of staff, provide technical assistance every step of the way. So simple a child could keep it going. With a percentage of the profits going to the corporation.

The first Sunset Nursing Home was established in Aldensville, and thrived. And again Wednesday afternoon was a busy time. Visitors from all over the state.

One morning in early June, in the nearby town of Clarksville, surrounded by his favorite kind of people—three doctors, two lawyers, and two bank officials—Joseph Eldon Hayworth slowly slumped forward on the table and took himself out of the nursing home business and all else.

A horde of hungry lawyers probed to see if perhaps a promising young corporation had also come to an untimely death. The Joseph Hayworth estate was scrutinized most carefully, while the family mourned.

Cletus arrived home a day late for the funeral. Turned loose from a jail in San Francisco. At about the time his father's coffin was being solemnly lowered into the ground, a jail guard, one of the two who had so happily knocked him about the cell the night before, came in to growl that his father was dead and he was being released.

Six months later, three weeks before Christmas, his mother died. Cletus missed that funeral, too. But only by four hours. Once again he looked into the angry and accusing eyes of his sister and brothers and had nothing to say except that he was sorry.

His father had, of course, left all his worldly possessions to his beloved wife, Hope. She, in turn, had left all her estate to her beloved children. But with certain stipulations.

She must have known when she entered the hospital for the operation that she likely would not be coming out alive. So she planned her will with great care.

At that time, with attorneys still working over the near-corpse of the corporation, bleeding it but keeping it alive, there wasn't much for the mother to leave. But for Walter, Paul, and Faith, there was five thousand dollars apiece. Cash. No stock was to be released yet.

For Cletus, nothing.

It had not been the mother's intention to deprive Cletus of his rightful share of the inheritance. It was only that she had wanted him to have it at the right time.

The will included the following conditions. First, Cletus would not get his inheritance until he would state in writing that he felt he was ready for it and able to use the money wisely. Second, his oldest brother, Walter, would have to attest that in his opinion Cletus was stable enough and mature enough to use the inheritance properly. Three, at the time that the first two conditions were met, Cletus would receive five thousand dollars, as his sister and brothers had received, and the remainder of the estate, including the stock, would be divided four ways among them so that in the final accounting the four children would all have received equal amounts.

It was a complicated and unusual will, but it held up in court.

The efforts of the lawyers were successful. Sunset Nursing Homes, Inc., not only survived, but thrived. More homes were established. Wednesday afternoons continued to bring a throng of well-dressed professional men who just happened to be looking around. The value of the stocks rose. Within two years after the mother's death the value was estimated at a quarter of a million dollars, and growing.

Walter, Paul, and Faith could hardly wait to get their hands on the money.

And Cletus wanted no part of it. He said that he did not feel that he could honestly state that he would be able to use it wisely.

Walter, Paul, and Faith groaned and swore. Faith not quite as much as the other two.

They told Cletus they thought he was now much more mature. Much more stable. And they pointed out the many things he could use the money for.

But he resisted, called their attention to the many examples of his instability and eccentricity, denied that he would use the money wisely. And besides, he had a psychiatrist who would certainly attest that he was not normal.

Walter, Paul, and Faith tried to be optimistic. They told one another that things were getting better. They recalled the day Cletus had come home late for his mother's funeral, his face bandaged, nose broken, shirt bloody. All the signs of his having been in a drunken brawl. And wasn't it true that nothing like that had happened since?

And remember the next day, the day after the funeral, when he had shown up at home in the late afternoon wearing an old miner's helmet. And how he had worn it around the house for a week. And how it had been two weeks before he had been willing to leave the house without it on his head.

They remembered how six months later, his first time back in Cranesville after enrolling in the state college in Farmington, he had got out of the car at Walter's house with the helmet on, refused to take it off during dinner, and afterwards got back into the car and driven off with the helmet still on his head.

And now he didn't wear it hardly at all. Only carried it with him when he visited.

So he was doing better and there was hope.

They would come into their full inheritance some day after all.

Chapter 5

The psychiatrist who Cletus asserted would certify that he was not normal was a Dr. Edmund Barber.

He was thirty-four years old, had been a classmate of Cletus's oldest brother, Walter, at the university. He was short, slender, balding, dark complexioned. He wore heavy, black-rimmed glasses that he took off and put back on every minute or so, a mannerism that gave an impression of being constantly on the alert. The mannerism did not inconvenience him because he saw as well without the glasses as with them. He had dark, piercing eyes that most patients found difficult to look directly into. This speeded up the point at which the patient was ready to start using the couch, thus accelerating the analytic process.

He was very successful and had an impressive waiting list of people eager to tell him what their problem was and what had happened that justified their having such a problem.

He looked forward to the day when he could grow a thick dark beard speckled with gray, which he would trim to a point. The waiting list he then would have would be so long as to warrant nationwide attention.

Dr. Barber had taken Cletus on as a client only because of his friendship with Walter. At no time, except possibly for a short period during the first session, did he consider Cletus to be good material for analysis. He did not consider the treatment a success. He did, in fact, terminate the case in what was unquestionably a most unprofessional manner.

As Cletus had said, Dr. Barber would have been happy to certify that the young man was not normal, though he would not have used that word. He might even have included his opinion that the man was not even likable. Among the many small things contributing to this conclusion was Cletus's insistence on wearing the miner's helmet before, during, and after each visit, thereby leading the patients in the waiting room to conclude that Dr. Barber dealt with a kind of mental case they did not like being associated with.

It had been Walter's idea that Cletus should see a psychiatrist. The responsibility for determining when and if Cletus should come into the money was one Walter wanted to share with another professional. Walter enlisted Faith's help in convincing Cletus that he should go. He would almost always agree to do what she asked. Payment, of course, would come from the estate.

That had been two years ago. The original schedule was for two visits a week. But Cletus missed the first appointment. And he missed the third and fifth. Dr. Barber astutely diagnosed this as a compulsion to be fair and equitable. One for you, one for me. So Dr. Barber suggested that if twice a week was too often, he would schedule only one visit a week. So Cletus came every two weeks.

Dr. Barber accepted that in silence. To agree that every two weeks was enough would have meant that he would see his young patient only thirteen times a year.

Cletus had arrived a few minutes late for his second scheduled visit, delayed by having met a friend he had not seen since high school, a friend now returned to Farmington to take a high executive position with the telephone company.

That story used up nearly five minutes. Dr. Barber took his glasses off and glanced at his watch with some impatience.

40

Ten more went for some wild excuse for having missed the first appointment. An obvious fabrication about his having been picked up by a young woman with a passion for sleeping with married men and how, after he had misled her into believing he was married, she had taken him to her apartment, wined and dined him, and made love to him in front of the television set.

Finally he got the young man to discuss his current situation. Then his childhood. Dr. Barber listened carefully for indications of early traumas.

Had he loved his father?

This brought out nothing especially significant. Mention of his father having been too busy at his business ventures to be the kind of companion a boy needed. And there was some resentment for small things such as being made to pay for candy at the store like any other boy.

Dr. Barber uncovered feelings that he doubted Cletus had been aware of. He resented, for example, his father having had himself adopted.

But enough of the father. Dr. Barber asked, "About your mother. Did you love your mother?"

There was a slight hesitation, and Barber waited.

"Only once."

Now the hesitation was on the part of the doctor. "I beg pardon?"

The statement was repeated. "Only once."

Cletus was lying on the couch, his helmet resting on his chest, his hands folded restfully on top of the helmet. Dr. Barber was behind him, out of sight.

"Would you like to say when this was?"

"You mean what time of day?"

Impatiently, "Of course not. I mean how old were you?"

Cletus said, "Fifteen, I think. Sixteen at the most."

Barber cleared his throat, knocked the ashes from his pipe into the ashtray, said, "Go ahead. Tell me about it."

There was some hesitation, a moment of uncertainty, before Cletus began. He took a deep breath and let the

41

air out slowly. "Father was away," he said. "He was at work tracing the family tree. He wanted to learn who his grandparents and great-grandparents were. His adoptive grand-parents and great-grandparents, that is."

Dr. Barber said, "Go ahead."

Cletus said, "He had gone on a two-day trip to Pownal, Vermont, where Reverend Hayworth's parents had come from. Checking old church records, that kind of thing. I recall it well because I remember Mother trying to persuade him not to go. She told him it wasn't that important who his adoptive grandparents were. But he insisted on going. He told her that family history was very important."

Dr. Barber said, "Go ahead."

"Mother was just getting over the flu. And I was coming down with it. But that, apparently, was not enough to keep him from checking out his ancestry."

Dr. Barber noted the tone of resentment in the young man's voice.

"It was early afternoon. My sister and brothers were at school. I was in bed. Mother didn't feel well and planned to go to her own bed. She was in her bathrobe. She stopped by to see how I felt."

He hesitated only a second, but Dr. Barber was right on him. Sharply, "Go ahead."

He said, "I had chills and was shaking. She lay down on the bed and tried to keep me warm. I was still shaking. She came under the covers with me, and said she'd stay until I fell asleep."

Dr. Barber was surprised that the young man could relate the story in such a calm voice. This might well have been the turning point in his life. "Go ahead."

Cletus said, "Mother was a beautiful woman. Taller than Father. Brunette. Clear white skin and dark eyes. Poised and graceful. I've never seen a woman walk with such grace. A quiet, gentle person. Very beautiful. I recall times when our family was swimming at the lake that I could see that my mother had a better figure than most women in their twenties."

Now there was a pause and Cletus seemed lost in memory. But Dr. Barber was ruthless. He said, "Get back to the story. Your mother was in bed with you."

So he continued, but seemingly with little enthusiasm. "As I said, I was feverish. So was she. We had both fallen asleep. I remember waking up on top of her. Her robe was open, and I was holding her breasts. And we were already in the act of making love."

A moment, then, "Actually, it was something that happened mostly in our sleep."

Dr. Barber permitted himself a quiet smile and an inaudible chuckle.

It always happens in their sleep!

"Go ahead."

Another long breath in and out before continuing. "I remember that even after we were awake and aware of what we were doing, we continued until we had finished. And it was very beautiful."

He repeated, "Very beautiful."

Already they had run beyond their allotted fifty minutes. But Dr. Barber did not rush his young patient out. He had too much admiration for one with courage enough to dredge up from his unconscious an experience as emotionally charged as the one he had just now unveiled. He took time for one question. "Have you ever told anyone of that incident? Anyone other than me?"

The boy said no.

Dr. Barber took time to jot some thoughts in the notebook, then closed it. "I'm sorry. But our time is up. Perhaps we can talk more about this next time."

Cletus got off the couch, shrugged his shoulders, said, "What else is there to say about it."

He put on his helmet and, without looking back, left the room.

He didn't show up for the next session anyway, and the one after that they talked of other matters.

Some weeks later, talking to Walter Hayworth and giving him a preliminary and tentative diagnosis, Dr. Barber mentioned Cletus's feelings about the adoptive family and his father's project to research the family tree.

Walter asked, "What family tree?"

"The one I mentioned. The adoptive family. I understand your father went out of state to where your grandfather and great-grandfather came from."

Walter said, "I don't think Father was interested in that kind of thing. Mostly he was just interested in business. Making money was what he liked to do. I suppose that if he had been interested in a family tree he would have hired someone to work it up for him."

Dr. Barber had his notebook in front of him. He turned a page. "About your mother. Cletus told me she was quite a beautiful woman."

Walter laughed softly. "No, Mother was hardly beautiful. Cletus must have meant that in the eyes of us, her children, she was a beautiful person. We loved her very much. But I don't think even we would say she was beautiful. She let herself get pretty fat, I'm afraid. In fact, it was a family joke about how she'd always say how some day she was going to go on a diet."

Dr. Barber checked his notes once more. "She was tall, wasn't she? And dark haired?"

Walter said, "No, she was sort of blond and very short. And heavy. She wouldn't have won any beauty prizes. But she was a great person, a good cook, housekeeper, and mother."

Then there was a small silence, after which Walter spoke again, this time with an apologetic tone to his voice.

He said, "Look, Ed, I think I understand what's happening. And I'm sorry I didn't tell you this earlier."

Barber said, "Tell me what?"

Walter said, "There's been a change in Cletus. You can't believe a damn thing he says any more."

Chapter 6

Cletus did not learn about the Greiner side of the family from his father. He learned about it from his cousin, Opal McCartney, a hard, belligerent, thirty-six-year-old mother of five. Short, with dark hair, angry eyes. Coy when she wished to be. She was the oldest daughter of his Aunt Martha, the one who had married the plumber's assistant. She had come to the office to say that she wanted to have all five of her children turned over to the state to care for. Cletus happened to be the one to interview her.

She started off with "I've had it!" and slammed her handbag down on the table in the small cubicle reserved for interviewing new cases.

"Drinking, fighting, gambling, swearing." And that was only the beginning.

"Drunk every Saturday, out of work every Monday. Hits me, beats the kids, spends his paycheck before he even gets home." She hit the table with her fist and repeated the initial summary: "I've had it."

Fairly routine so far, and Cletus poised his pencil over the application form. He asked her name. She said, "Opal Greiner McCartney. Greiner was my maiden name."

The name meant nothing to him. He asked for the husband's name, address, names and ages of all the children, and family background. She provided all he asked for.

"I can't take it any more. Not with that man around the house. I want the state to take all my kids and put them in foster homes."

45

She dug into the handbag for a handkerchief. "The sonofabitch is out of work more than he's working." She blew her nose. "And pardon my French."

He said, "That's all right." Then, "How long has it been like this?"

"All our married life. Long as I can remember."

He said, "Too bad," and shook his head sympathetically. "Maybe it's time you got rid of him."

That was what she was going to do. "Right now. Put all the kids in foster homes and then leave him."

That made sense. "You can always find some place to go," he said. "With relatives or someone. Or go to work."

"I'd live with a sister, probably. Or one of my brothers."

"Then that's probably what you ought to do." And that sounded like a final decision. "How many brothers and sisters do you have?"

She said three brothers and two sisters, and he said, "Really? That's a big family."

She thought he sounded critical. "I like big families."

He said, "Me, too. There were seven of us. I think big families are wonderful."

Her expression softened. So they had something in common. "I'm the oldest."

"I'm the youngest!" And she said, "Well!" and gave him a nice warm smile.

He smiled back.

He leaned back in his chair, relaxed, formality temporarily set aside. "Big families do have more problems, though," he said. "Like my second oldest brother was killed in Vietnam, and my oldest sister lost a leg in an automobile accident." He added, philosophically, "If you have big families you got big worries."

She knew what he meant. One of her sisters lost a husband in the war.

"Both my parents are dead," he said.

"I'm sorry."

"Both yours alive?"

46

She said they both were, and crossed herself. "Thanks to God." And she knocked on wood to make doubly sure. "People live to an old age in my family. My grandfather died only last year. He was ninety-two."

Cletus looked amazed. And happy for her and for her deceased grandfather.

She was enjoying this chat. Such a nice young man!

"He was a Greiner," she said. "Had five children." Then she paused, looked closely at him for a moment. "Where you from?"

He said, "Pennsylvania. Pittsburgh, Pennsylvania. My father was a coal miner. One of the best, they tell me. Died when I was very small. Mine cave-in."

She said, "Oh. I thought you might be from Cranesville." And he asked why did she think that.

She said she had an uncle there. Her mother's brother. A Joe Greiner who had run away from home when he was only fourteen and had been adopted and had his name changed to Hayworth. "When you first told me your name I thought of that. Because you look something like the Greiners do."

He drew it all out of her. The whole family tree. And he sat there fascinated. It was like going back to the old home town that you'd never seen. Back to familiar places you'd never heard of. He asked what they were like, where they lived. What they did. It turned out that he knew two of George's boys. He had played pool with them at Sandy's Bar and Grill more than once. One of them owed him five dollars that he knew he would never collect.

She included the story about the time her grandfather, seventy-five years old, who had come on hard times, had gone to Cranesville and seen his son, who owned a big drugstore, and had asked him for a little money to tide him over.

"What happened, for God's sake?"

She said, "Nothing. He got nothing." She shook her

head. "His own son, who he'd raised, turned him down."

"How could he have done that!"

She said, in the special tone reserved for family gossip, "His son told him that he'd made a decision twenty-five years ago and intended to stick to it."

Cletus was impressed. He nodded several times. "That must have taken a lot of courage."

She said, "My grandfather had a lot of courage. I'll say that for him."

That wasn't what Cletus had meant. But he let it pass.

She told him about her own children, some of whom were either in trouble or on their way to it. Her oldest daughter, April, had stayed out of school so much she almost got sent away. And sometimes stayed out all night. Cletus offered to talk to her if she would come in to see him.

Then he got down to business, for he didn't intend to take any five kids into care.

He said, "Which of your family do you think you would move in with?" And while she thought about it, he offered some advice. "Usually moving in with a brother is best. At least, that's the way it was with my sister, who had a problem like yours. She had only three children, though, and you have five." He explained that she had tried living with a sister and it didn't work. "Then she moved to a brother's house and things went much better."

He said, "Her problem was much like yours. Married to a man who drank." He shook his head, remembering. "When he did work, he was the best worker you could find. But the poor bastard wouldn't hold on to a job."

Then, quickly, "Pardon the language. That slipped out!"

She laughed and put a hand gently on his arm. "Look," she said, "my language isn't always so good either," and they both laughed.

"He wasn't a bad fellow, actually," Cletus said. "Lots

48

of fun at a party or picnic. Big hearty laugh. Everybody liked him."

She said, "You just described my Stanley to a T." She touched his arm once more.

"Have a family gathering on Sunday, with something to drink," Cletus said, "and George wouldn't be in shape for work Monday. And there goes another job." He made a gesture like a bomb exploding.

"God! Oh, my God, so true!" She threw up her hands. "You've hit Stanley right on the nose. My God, that's him. Great fun at a picnic, but there goes another job."

They laughed together for a long moment. Then he grew serious.

He said, "I think she was satisfied with George as far as their sex life was concerned."

She had no complaint in that regard, either.

He said, "I'm glad to say that things finally worked out all right for my sister, Lois. Though it was bad for a while. She moved in with my brother, Clarence, and his family, but that got awkward after a while. And she couldn't get a job that she could enjoy." He added, "With my family, getting together with them for a big picnic is one thing. Trying to live with them over a period of time is another."

That was true of her family, too.

"What my sister finally did," he confided, "—though I'm not suggesting this is related to your situation—was to go back to him and work things out. And I must admit that my sister had been partly to blame. She nagged at George more than she was willing to admit. And his way to get even with her was to make her angry by drinking and losing jobs. At least that was the opinion of her marriage counselor. It was a thing they had going between them. She would nag, he would drink. She would make him angry, he would make her angry to get even.

"She took a different attitude finally. A kind of cold-blooded attitude. He was the source of income. Her only source of income. So she kind of nurtured him, talked
49

nice to him, kept him working. She did nice things to get him to work overtime, even. They bought a house and the poor devil now is working night and day to pay for it. To please the sweet little wife at home."

Cletus laughed for a moment at that. Or at something. Then got serious again. "But I've spent all the time so far talking about my family and haven't spent much time on what you came here to talk about." He turned his attention back to the application form.

She looked thoughtful. There were some good things she hadn't mentioned. The kids were in good health and generally happy. Stanley would be working again in a few days, probably. "Construction," she said. "Heavy equipment. Makes good money when he works."

Cletus said, "You're lucky to have a husband with that kind of skill."

She agreed. "When I see other women's husbands, I sometimes think I'm lucky to have a husband who works even *sometimes*."

Cletus moved the application form to the side. "It won't be easy," he told her. "Husbands like Stanley are hard to get along with. You've got to put lots of work into it. That's what my sister discovered. Keep him happy. Don't nag him. You know what I mean? Make him realize that it's important he keep bringing in that money to keep you and the children and himself happy. And buy a house as soon as you find one you like."

It seemed to make sense to her.

He dropped the application form into the wastebasket. "But come back if things don't go well."

She said she would. And thanked him. "And when you see your sister in Pittsburgh, tell her I'm glad things worked out so well for her."

He said that he'd probably be seeing her next weekend, and he'd tell her. "And send April in and I'll talk to her about staying in school and coming home nights."

She said she would. And she did.

50

April McCartney was fifteen, with long reddish hair, mischievous eyes, a flippant sense of humor, and not a serious thought in her head. She had green eyes, a small well-shaped body, and in a very short time a deep crush on one Cletus Hayworth. She had a poor school record, a boyfriend with the bad habit of stealing cars, and nothing about her that softened the heart of the juvenile court justice, the Honorable Samuel Gamboli. Only the intercession of Cletus Hayworth kept her from being sent to the Holy Mary Home for Girls. Cletus told Judge Gamboli that he planned to counsel her regularly and would guarantee success for her in home, school, and community. Gamboli ordered her case continued for six months with the provision that she see Mr. Hayworth regularly once a week.

Nothing could have pleased her more. Unless maybe regularly each day.

He kept her at arm's length, and the desk between them, except when sometimes they'd walk to the Dairy Queen and buy cones and eat them as they walked back to the office. Or drive out to the lake and sit and talk.

He talked to her like an uncle, which he was.

"What surprises me about you and your friends is that you think of yourself as young rebels. And there isn't a one of you who's rebelled against anything?"

She said, "Hah. What do you think I am? A virgin?"

"I never considered that to be very likely."

"You can always find out for yourself, if you want." And she swung her hips as she walked. She licked the ice cream cone and looked provocatively up at him.

He said, "I don't intend to. So quit bringing up the subject."

After a moment he said, "Ask your mother, and she'll tell you that you are at fifteen exactly the way she was at fifteen. Just as your brother, Pat, is the image of what his father was at that age."

"So?"

"So you're not rebels. Not a one of you. There's not

51

one of your friends who's done anything different from the way your parents did it."

He said, "For you to rebel would be for you to try to like school, plan to finish and maybe go to college."

"No chance!"

"Of course not. You're just a follower. If you were a rebel, you'd make up your own mind about school. And about teachers, police, social workers."

She said, "I like social workers. One, anyway."

"You're simply following the family pattern." He said, "There isn't a single idea you have that you arrived at by your own thinking."

He looked down at her, not without affection. "I wish you were a rebel. It would be good for you."

This kind of talk got neither of them anywhere. She kept on being like all the Greiners he'd ever met. For the boys, drop out of school and buy a secondhand car and stay broke trying to keep it going. For the girls, drop out of school and attach yourself to some boy who is staying broke trying to keep his secondhand car running.

Once he got partly into a discussion of fabrication, but pulled out when he found she couldn't follow the reasoning involved.

He accused her of lying to him about going to school the day before. But she said it wasn't a lie. She had gone to school, but decided, after she got there, to cut the first class. And then decided to skip the rest, too.

He said it was a lie, or at least an intentionally misleading statement. Not just a fabrication. It didn't qualify as a fabrication, he explained, "because it was a matter of some significance to me. Because it is my responsibility to see that you go to school." He said, "If, for instance, you had told me your math teacher came to school wearing sandals, that would have been a fabrication. Can you see the difference?"

"No."

He said, "It's because it is of no interest to me whether

52

your math teacher wore sandals to class. Or even no shoes at all."

On this occasion they were sitting by the lake looking over the water.

She said, "Me either." And laughed lightly, kicked off her own sandals and wiggled her toes.

"Telling a fabrication," he said, "can have a useful result. For instance, I bet that tomorrow you look to see what kind of shoes your math teacher is wearing. Also, knowing the difference between a fabrication and a lie gives you a better understanding of what is significant and what is not."

She was mostly just watching her toes move, probably not really listening. But he went on. "It can also help keep a little distance between you and people you've got to occasionally stand a little apart from. For instance, if your math teacher seems to be crowding you too much, bugging you, go up to him sometime and say, 'I met a boy last week who used to go to school here and he asked if you were still teaching.' Tell him that the boy was in town to see his family before leaving for Lakeview, Nebraska, to take a big job with the telephone company. And if he asks you the name of the boy just say you forgot."

She asked, "What good would that do?"

He said, "You won't know until you try it. But I'll tell you this, it will make you feel a little less awed by him. Your relationship with him will be easier. And it will make you aware that you don't know anyone who is on his way to Nebraska to work for the telephone company."

She didn't even know where Nebraska was.

He said, "Don't get hung up on truth. Nothing is sacred, not even the truth. Play around with it until you can tell when you're telling the truth as you know it, and when you're only repeating something you were told is true. Something you never questioned."

What she wanted him to say was that the truth was that he was suddenly feeling very passionate, and desired her very much. And would she come back to the car so they could drive to some secluded place where they could be alone.

"Sometime, when you're talking with someone you'll likely not see again, tell him your father is a bus driver. The man will not know or care. But for the first time you will be really aware that your father is not a bus driver."

He glanced down at her. "By the way. What *does* your father do for a living?"

She didn't really know. "Takes jobs when he can get them, I suppose."

She put her sandals back on. She was bored with this kind of talk. "Can we go now?"

So the seed of the idea he was working out in his mind had in this case fallen on barren ground. But he didn't give up. Later, he tried it on his sister, Faith. But the results were inconclusive. He thought it worked. She didn't.

As for April, she figured in the Mary Kalinski case in a small but devastating way.

What she did, actually, was really screw it up.

of City Hall. That incident was reported on page one. And three hundred students at the high school signed a petition making Cletus and his friend honorary heroes of the year.

There were other things.

The day she was assigned the lead in the high school senior class play and hurried to tell her father at the store, she found him too much distracted to pay her much attention. Cletus had been suspended that day for wearing his hair too long. And he refused to cut it. And the school refused to let him back in until he did. Her father had had to go to the school committee and threaten legal action in order to get his son back in.

Another thing.

She wasn't allowed out after midnight until she was eighteen years old.

Cletus came in any time he wanted to, almost.

And more.

In her senior year in high school she was not allowed to go with her class on a three-day trip to New York City because her father thought it too dangerous.

Two months later Cletus went to a music festival at Woodstock, New York, with a girl friend, and for three days they slept on the ground, almost starved, swam naked in muddy ponds, smoked marijuana, mingled with drug addicts and hippies from San Francisco, came home and told all about it.

So their monthly meetings were not without a certain tension. Sometimes more than others. And the night she went to Farmington to the concert at the college was one of the more strained occasions. It ended with her getting very angry and walking out on him.

After the concert they had gone to the student lounge, where over soda and potato chips they had exchanged notes on their respective well-being, and she had reported on the members of the family back in Cranesville.

He had his helmet with him, but carried it as inconspicuously as possible, as if sensitive of her feelings regarding it.

For her it had been a hard day at the store. Things had happened that had drained her patience. And his having arrived a few minutes late with a story about an old friend from Brandeis who was passing through town on his way to Hollywood to direct a documentary film on the American Indian had only increased her irritation.

He asked about Grandmother Hayworth.

She responded sharply that she had never before heard him refer to her as Grandmother Hayworth. "Do you have more than one?"

Then, without waiting for a reply, she said, "Never mind. Anyway, she's fine."

He said, "Good. And the aunt who lives with you? Suddenly I forget her name."

She felt a flood of anger. "Cletus, you know you don't really care. So why do you ask?"

He answered honestly enough, and with some show of annoyance himself. "I don't know. Out of some misguided sense of politeness, I suppose. Nothing more."

She felt depressed. And sorry she had driven all the way from Cranesville to see him.

The people at the table behind her were talking too loudly about a party the night before. An all-night party, apparently, with emphasis on who had ended up with whom. Their conversation bothered her very much. She almost turned and requested that they lower their voices.

"You seem tired tonight," Cletus said. "The store getting you down?"

She snapped back, "Of course not." And for a moment or two they were both silent.

At the table on her left the subject was ecology. Or maybe philosophy. Two boys and a girl. The girl said, "The trouble with you two is that you're overimpressed with the fact that you were born as human beings."

Cletus said, "It's not important, and I don't know why
58

I mention it. But the reason I happened to ask about our grandmother and aunt is because they happened to be in a dream I had last night. So they happened to be on my mind."

She didn't say anything. Hearing other people's dreams was not her idea of stimulating conversation.

He said, "You want to hear it."

"Sure." What else could you say?

The girl at the next table added, "If you had happened to have been assembled as a frog or a tree, you would see things from a different point of view."

Cletus said, "You . . ." The rest of the sentence was drowned out by laughter from the boys.

"I didn't hear you."

He repeated, "You were in it too."

She said, "Oh."

He said, "You'd got home from work and had fixed yourself a drink. Maybe more than one. And you had lit a cigarette and had strolled casually into where they were sitting." He said, "I remember you strolled up to Grandmother, kind of relaxed, smiling, and asked how she had been feeling. And she'd said, 'Pretty good.'"

She hoped it hadn't been a long dream. There was a limit to how long she could pretend to be interested.

"You asked how well she was fixed financially, and she said, 'Well enough.'"

Cletus looked as if he was trying to remember the exact words. "I think you said, 'Able to take care of all conceivable emergencies?' (or something like that). And she said, 'Yes.'"

Faith wished they'd gone someplace where they could have had a drink. She had recently taken to having a glass of wine when she was out. A glass now would taste good.

"You asked Aunt Edna and got the same answers. And then you stood there for a moment, looking at both of them. You said that things seemed to be going well for them. And they agreed."

59

He said—and she was glad to note that he seemed to be coming to the end—"You walked over and gently put a hand on their shoulders, gently, lovingly, smiled at them, and said that everything seemed to be all right. So you thought you'd be moving on." He finished with, "And you left."

There was a long pause. She could only assume that he had now finished. Which he had. And she was not impressed.

"Is that all?"

He said, "Yes. Except that at the end was the sound of you getting into your Oldsmobile and driving off."

She didn't laugh. She felt sad rather than amused. She said, "I suppose the dream symbolized your rejection of responsibility. Your belief that people should walk away from their burdens."

She saw a hurt expression cloud his face and in an instant her feelings changed. She didn't want to hurt him. Her crazy, mixed-up brother whom she had admired and fought against all her life. She said, quickly, "I'm sorry. I didn't mean that the way it sounded."

He accepted her apology. Maybe accepted it too quickly. And immediately she felt herself swinging back the other way. She looked at him hard, and said, "But it's true. And you *know* it. You have *never* accepted responsibility."

Example after example flashed into mind.

The girl at the next table was continuing her argument with the two boys. She was saying that something or other was not true. "Man," she said, "will *not* prevail. He'll be lucky even to survive. And he'll survive only if he doesn't try to *prevail.*" She added, in apparently what was a heavy conversation, "If the blue whale goes, we will too!"

Cletus said, "I have great respect for family responsibilities. But I think a family should be a source of strength and happiness, not an enclosure."

The word enclosure hit her ears and hurt. Never had

60

his family been an enclosure. He had no right to imply that it had. The thoughts that had been charging through her mind all evening now burst into the open. "No one ever asked you to be enclosed. All anyone asked was that you show a little responsibility." She said, "You've never *known* responsibility. I *have.* I've managed the family business for four years!" She said, "I've had the responsibility for arranging funerals you've not even been responsible enough to be present at."

She was about to cry.

And Cletus had the helmet in a lightning flash up on the table and his hand was on it, ready.

That made her even more furious. The helmet. The childish defense against reality. His way of blocking off what people were saying. But it wouldn't work this time. She raised her voice until it was almost a shout.

"It's true, Cletus. And you know it. You *know* it!"

He didn't say anything, just kept his hand on the helmet, his eyes straight into hers. She said it a third time. "You know it. You know very well that when I should have been at the funeral home, consoling Mother, I was on the phone trying to find someone in San Francisco who knew where you were."

And in a lower voice, "And you were in jail for burning a flag or something. And I had to hire a lawyer all the way across the United States to get you out."

She had her handkerchief out. The next lines were from behind the handkerchief, muffled, words seeming to be addressed to herself more than to him. Words shooting up from the deep well of memory, recalled in anguish, flung out from the tortured pit of her weary soul. Impersonal. Meant only to be released, not to hurt. "And that morning that you came home four hours late for your mother's funeral, getting out of that taxi and coming up the walk, your nose broken and blood all over you. Looking like some drunken bum coming home after an all-night brawl!"

61

Then, softer, bitterly, "And all you could say was that you were sorry."

And she broke down and wept.

It was half a minute or more before she opened her eyes. And looked at him.

He sat there with his helmet on. His face gone blank. And she could hear that around them the room had grown silent.

She was filled with rage, but she kept her voice low. She said, "Take it off, Cletus."

But he didn't. He only stared straight at her, defiantly, his eyes like the holes of two dark cannons guarding the castle against intruders.

"Take it off right now."

And no response.

She said, "Take if off, or I'm leaving."

And still no move.

She quietly gathered her cigarettes, pocketbook, and jacket. She daubed once more at her eyes, got up, and, with what dignity she could manage, left the room.

Chapter 8

One would be justified in holding to the belief that the turning point in the life of Cletus Hayworth was his meeting with Heidi Zimmerman. The reason for this is that she was the dominant factor in the series of events that led to his being late for his mother's funeral.

Heidi. Cheerful, reddish blond, stocky, with freckles. Very independent. Played a good game of pool, could hike for miles, whip up a meal out of almost nothing at all. Fix plumbing. She could chop wood. You would expect that she would major in animal psychology, marry a forestry major, and they would buy acreage in Maine and raise animals and cut down trees and write books. Which might well be what she ended up doing. But when Cletus found her she was into a different trip.

Cletus, still smelling of tear gas from the troops guarding the Pentagon, met her on Pennsylvania Avenue near the White House after the peace marchers had disbanded. It was early evening. He was happy to see that there was something about him she liked. It might have been only the smell of tear gas, but it was enough. He had his sleeping bag next to hers that night, and the next morning they left together for Colorado to see some former classmates of his. They were there two weeks. They came back to New York to stay with some friends of hers, and there she heard from other friends in Boston, Massachusetts, about a mass demonstration and sit-in at the Department of Welfare, sponsored by the Welfare Rights Organization. The organization was demanding that families on welfare get a flat grant of money to cover special needs rather than having the department provide money for such needs as they arose. Or perhaps it was the other way around. Whichever way it was, it turned out that the change was made and then later returned to what it had been originally. But that has no bearing on what happened.

They stayed in New York long enough to join the march on the United Nations protesting American support for the dictatorship in Greece. Then they left the city.

That was in early December. They arrived in Boston in time for the first heavy snowfall of winter. In time for Heidi and him to join the march and the sit-in.

In Cranesville that day the snow was falling also. Eight inches had put a white hush on the landscape. In the waiting room of Memorial Hospital a distraught Walter Hayworth walked to where Paul and Faith were seated and solemnly broke the news that their mother was dying. He said it might be only hours. Days at the most.

It proved to be only hours.

And everyone said, "Poor family. Only six months after Mr. Hayworth died."

Walter asked Faith to take on the task of finding Cletus. And she didn't know where to begin. She had written to him a week ago in care of a friend in New York City, and yesterday the letter had been returned with the notation that the addressee had moved and had left no forwarding address.

Walter said he didn't care if they ever found him.

Paul said he didn't care if they even tried.

Faith, in tears, called everyone she knew who had ever known him. No one knew where to start looking. A former roommate of his at Brandeis, Sidney Weysmith, in Boston, had heard he'd gone to Colorado. He later called to correct this, saying a friend recently back from New

64

York said he'd seen him there. Then the morning of the funeral, only an hour before the family was to assemble at the church, Sidney called one last time to say he'd picked up a copy of the Boston *Globe* and thought he recognized Cletus in the picture of the demonstrators in the welfare office in Boston. He wasn't sure. But the one standing next to the stocky girl in front of the door to the commissioner's office looked a lot like him.

And it was. Faith called Boston and a police officer was sent to break the news.

The weather in Boston wasn't suitable for picketing, but it was ideal for sitting in. The corridor leading to the welfare commissioner's office was wide and long and there was room for the nearly one hundred demonstrators to stretch their legs and spread out. There were bathrooms down the hall, left unlocked so the young people could use them.

They were quite young, most of them, and from varied backgrounds. About two-thirds were white. The remainder were mostly black, with a scattering of Puerto Ricans. About a third were girls, almost all of them white. Most girls were with male companions. Most of the demonstrators were either in college or college dropouts. Only a small minority were from families on welfare. The ones in best spirits were the ones from out of town.

Friends from outside brought in coffee, doughnuts, and sandwiches. Several had guitars, so there was music and song, laughs, jokes, good humor. Any funny remark was passed down or up the corridor until everyone had had a chance to hear it.

There were TV cameras and newspaper reporters. The only thing missing was a TV set so they could see themselves on the six-thirty news.

Every time a photographer's flashbulb went off everyone cheered.

Cletus and Heidi had a good spot right in front of the door to the commissioner's office. The commissioner, sensibly enough, had stayed away.

The police were there. Word was passed along that there were a large number of cops in a room around the corner, keeping out of sight. But never at any one time were there more than two policemen in view, and they had been carefully selected for the job.

Always one was white and one was black. Always young, quiet, smiling, friendly, joking. In two-hour shifts the pair would walk the length of the corridor, keeping a path clear for the commissioner who never showed up. Always careful to avoid stepping on anyone's feet or saying anything to evoke an angry response. They smiled at insults, listened to the guitar music and applauded at the end of each song. Sometimes they would let themselves get drawn into discussions, always showing a certain amount of sympathy for the cause the demonstrators were supporting. One black cop said, "Look, man. My mother's on welfare right now!"

One young rookie said his name was Mike Devanny, and with a reluctance that was either real or done with considerable acting ability, asking his buddy for God's sake to keep an eye out for the sergeant, borrowed a guitar and played—not too well, but with good feeling—two Woody Guthrie songs from the depression era.

The police thing was handled so well that it took much of the spirit and almost all of the anger out of the demonstration. The group almost left at the end of the day. A few did. But the rest remained. Because outside it was snowing, and with the girls here the men wanted to keep the party going. A few bottles of wine had showed up. One bearded young man held his bottle up, kept his arm around his girl, and said, "Shit, man! I got everything I need." And everyone laughed or cheered.

So they got through the night. The cops didn't need to keep the path open, so there was plenty of room. Even so, some people's legs got in other people's way.

But some men had women and some didn't, and there was some irritation because of this.

And outside the snow continued to fall. From the window the scene was so peaceful it was almost like Christmas.

In the morning more coffee and doughnuts were brought in. And that was good. But two men had some angry words over a girl, and that was bad. There were tensions building and some changing of positions. Sections of the corridor took on a more homogeneous appearance. Most of the college people and the members of the Welfare Rights Organization stayed near the door to the commissioner's office. Cletus and Heidi stayed with this part of the group.

The blacks bunched up halfway down the corridor. And toward the end were the Puerto Ricans, the ones from families actually on welfare, and others who looked as if they wanted to be near the doors in case there was trouble.

But it didn't seem there would be any trouble. The rumor started that the commissioner simply didn't intend to come to the office until the crowd got tired and hungry and went home. Today no effort was made to keep the path clear. A feeling of futility began to take hold, and frustration led to worse language and louder threats of what would happen to the commissioner if he did dare try to get to his office. One man got tired of hearing the obscenities, got up and took his girl and left. There were some catcalls, but most of the criticism was directed at those using the foul language.

The young rookie, Mike Devanny, was back with his black partner. They just stood at the end of the corridor and didn't try to walk into the crowd. Someone asked Devanny if he were going to play the guitar today and he said he was afraid that the sergeant might catch him at it.

There were some jokes and laughs and a few songs, but by midmorning it was clear that today wasn't going to be as much fun as yesterday had been.

Then the sergeant and a lieutenant appeared at the end of the corridor and talked with the two young cops. The lieutenant pointed toward the door to the commissioner's office, and a moment later the young cops began making their way down the corridor.

So maybe the commissioner was going to show up after all. Perhaps now there would be some action and the long night's discomfort might have been worth it.

The two made their way slowly, with the crowd separating enough to let them pass, but closing immediately in their wake. The group was simply being nice to the two young officers, not making a path for the commissioner. And everybody waited for the action.

There were some good-natured remarks about the characteristics of cops in general. Some a bit more personal and not so good-natured. But the young men in uniform kept smiling—stepping carefully—and occasionally saying excuse me—and made it halfway. From the end of the corridor the sergeant and lieutenant watched.

From one side came "motherfuckers," and the cops turned their heads. A foot got in the way of the black cop, either overlooked or put there intentionally, and he fell. He fell on top of a black girl. And when she cried out in pain it was like a shot of adrenalin and along the line muscles tensed and the blood sped a little faster.

A man swore and pushed the cop off the girl, but the man from the other side pushed back and the black rookie again fell, this time his nightstick sinking point first into the girl's stomach.

The agonizing and prolonged scream that then erupted cried out for revenge. Someone kicked at the cop's face and he lashed back with his stick. And tried to get to his feet.

Someone shouted, "Get his gun." And some damn fool did just that.

Behind him, the white cop was down and someone had grabbed his stick. He kicked out with heavy service shoes and a white girl threw a hand to her bloodied mouth and

68

her scream joined that of the black girl. For a long moment the discord of these separate howls of pain split the air, accompanied by yells of anger and threats and curses.

Then there was sudden silence. The screams of both girls subsided abruptly and dropped to barely audible sobs. All eyes were on the scene in the center of the stage.

In the middle of the corridor, in a space that had suddenly opened, a tall thin black with an Afro hairdo and a thin wisp of beard crazily waved the service revolver, slowly, mockingly, in front of the young black cop, crouched on one knee before him.

Half a dozen feet away the other rookie, Devanny, was almost on his feet. And at the end of the corridor other cops had come running up. But, mostly, eyes were on that small black hole at the end of the barrel of the gun two feet from the frightened face of the officer it belonged to.

The black rookie had no choice. With your people watching, you don't let someone take your gun from you. Not and be a man. So he jumped. He jumped just as Devanny rose to his feet. And just as the lieutenant fired from fifty feet away.

For the first few seconds the only blood that spilled was what spurted from the side of the white cop's head. After that, as six officers charged down the corridor, it flowed copiously from the side of the black with the Afro hairdo who had toppled with the lieutenant's second shot, from the heads of long-haired boys with no place to run, from the mouths of girls who tried to flatten themselves against the wall.

Clubs cracked indiscriminately against heads and bodies, boy and girl, young and younger.

Cletus saw them coming, still coming, lashing out in fury at all who got in their way. The sergeant had grabbed a nightstick and drove more furiously than any other, charging even past the group knotted about the fallen officer, hitting at everything that moved, right up to where Cletus, his body in front of Heidi, shielding her, could only stand and wait.

The sergeant was so close that his hot breath was like a blast from hell and his contorted face like a tortured demon's. His huge left hand grabbed Cletus hard by the collar and he screamed.

"You goddamned son of a bitchin' long-haired bastard your mother's dead!"

And the raised club came smashing down.

Chapter 9

About the helmet.

The old section of Cranesville, down around River Street and First, is the place to walk for a man with a troubled mind. Cletus walked there the day after his mother's funeral.

This is the section where the old tannery is. The tannery is the ancient, abandoned building, brick, windows boarded up. Falling down, almost. Rusted iron spiked fence all around the grounds. In the summer the high grass and weeds and the dirt and peeling paint give it an air of pathetic desolation. But in the winter, covered with fresh snow, the ugliness is hidden and the old building has a certain grandeur.

A little ways north is the city dump. Nothing very romantic about that, even covered over by snow. So Cletus didn't go in that direction. Just once around the tannery and up First, back toward Main Street.

The sky was filled with clubs crashing down and the air filled with angry voices telling him that it had all been his fault.

And his face ached. It ached with every step he took. And he had walked a long way.

The snow had stopped. It was bitter cold.

Heading back toward town, on the corner, just before you get to the row of secondhand shops, is a small grocery store. In front of the store was a newspaper rack, and the afternoon edition of the Cranesville *Courier* was on display.

The headlines were about what Cletus had expected.

TWO DEAD, EIGHT HURT IN WELFARE RIOT

The police officer, according to the story, had died early this morning, raising the death toll to two. Eight demonstrators were still hospitalized. The trouble had started when the mob got out of control and had attacked the police.

Nothing was said of an officer sent to deliver a message of a death in the family.

On the front page was a picture of Officer Devanny.

The miner's helmet was in the window of the second-hand shop next to the grocery store. He spotted it there among the old dishes, table lamps, used waffle irons, used radios, statues of the Virgin Mary.

The helmet cost a dollar. Cletus wore it home.

He didn't take it off for a week except to sleep. It was two weeks before he was able to leave home without it.

Chapter 10

Not all the times that Faith and Cletus met did it end as unpleasantly as the occasion of the concert at the college. That particular evening, actually, was after a while remembered with amusement by both of them. They laughed about it.

Gradually they got together more often, more enjoyably. There was one evening when she met him at Sandy's, drank wine, and even at one point put on his silly helmet.

That was the night—to put it in its chronological sequence—just before the morning Cletus got the Mary Kalinski case.

It was a quiet night at Sandy's. No one had shouted at anyone, hardly. No one had thrown anything.

They had been reminiscing of high school and early college days. Amicably. She had confided that she had been secretly pleased about his getting arrested for painting peace signs on the old Civil War cannon. Proud of him, that is. Not glad that he'd been arrested. And he had said that he had been proud of her being elected president of the student council in her junior year. It had freed him, in a way. Her having won certain kinds of honors left him free to try things in different areas.

"Do you understand what I mean?"

She said, "I think I do."

He said, "If I had been the older, I would have been on the high honor role every year, as you were, and you would have been free to get pregnant at sixteen and get busted for smoking grass."

So that was a small laugh. Not very big, but they shared it. She said, "Thanks. But at least I would have got to go to Woodstock that summer instead of staying home and helping in the store."

But that wasn't fair, she admitted. "I could have gone if I'd wanted to. I can't blame you because I didn't do anything very exciting."

There was a short, thoughtful silence. Then he said, "I remember writing to you from San Francisco and suggesting you come out."

She remembered.

"Why didn't you?"

She wasn't sure. "I suppose the idea didn't really interest me that much. There was another place I would have gone to, if I could have gone anywhere."

He asked where that was, and she didn't answer right away. She smiled ruefully, and let her mind make its way back those four years. "It was so long ago," she said. "It's hardly worth mentioning."

He said that it hadn't been so long ago.

"It seems like it." And she laughed lightly but not happily.

He persisted. Where was it she would have gone?

She gave in. "I'll tell you, but remember that it happened a long time ago and doesn't bother me any more."

He promised to remember that.

And she reminded him of something he'd forgotten. That there had been a student she had known during her junior year at college. Cletus had met him. Man named Sam Fredo, a senior. Big, simple fellow. Huge feet; clumsy looking but wasn't. Very bright. Unpretentious, with a quiet wit. Played the guitar.

"Someone I'd met on a geological field trip. He was leaving for graduate school in Colorado in the fall."

Cletus said, "I remember. He came home with you once."

She pressed her cigarette into the ashtray. She said, "He'd talked me into transferring to Colorado State University for my senior year so we could be together."

And though it was hardly necessary, she added, "We were very fond of each other. But the timing was wrong."

She wanted to end the story there, but he kept after her. She kept saying that he would take it too seriously, and that it had happened a long time ago. Anyway, as she had said, it didn't bother her any more.

The rest of the story was that she had gone to her father after coming home from school at the end of her junior year and told him she had decided not to work in the drugstore after all. That she wanted to go to Colorado and finish college. Study geology. And there had been hard words exchanged.

"We talked about it at breakfast," Faith said. "Which wasn't the best place or time of day for a serious discussion. He didn't have much time to talk about it because he had an appointment to meet some people in Clarksville that morning."

She took a cigarette from the pack and lit it. "I know I shouldn't have said the things I did. But neither should he. He said I had made an agreement and had to stick to it. And I told him what I thought of him and his damn drugstore."

Cletus had the helmet on the seat beside him. He moved it over into his lap, but still out of sight.

"Anyway, he said I had no right to change my mind. That I had to stick to my agreement. But he'd be willing to talk about it some more after he got back." And she paused for a moment.

"Afterwards, after he'd gone, Mother told me I shouldn't talk to my father like that. That I might be sorry."

She finished with, "You can probably guess what morning that was. And what happened."

His hands gripped the helmet hard.

Knocking the cigarette against the ashtray, not looking

at him, she said, "Go ahead. Put it on if you want to."

"No. It's all right."

There was more. She felt she might as well tell that, too, now that she'd got started.

She said, "Sam kept writing to me from Colorado." And for a moment she was silent, as if quietly deciding to skip past some parts that might as well be left out. "By December I'd decided once again that I wanted to go. I had been managing the store. It wasn't as difficult as I had thought it would be. We could easily hire someone to manage it for us. In fact I'd found just the person. When I told Walter, he thought it was probably all right. But ask mother."

He heard what sounded like the light hum of bees. Or maybe many voices in the distance. He couldn't distinguish the words, but the tone was angry. Something flew past his head and he brushed at it.

"So I talked to Mother, but she didn't like the idea. She made me promise not to do anything about it until she got back from the hospital. And to take care of Grandmother and Aunt Edna until she got home."

He slammed the helmet on his head just in time.

They came on like endless waves of bombers hurling nightsticks the size of telephone poles almost, with a chorus of angry voices shouting that it was somehow all his fault. Blows rained upon his thin helmet like fists, and he could only huddle there waiting for it to end.

She said, "It's all right. I don't mind."

She sat there, shoulders slumped, a single tear slowly making its way down her cheek. She took in a deep breath and released it slowly.

He did the only thing an honorable man could do. He took the helmet off and held it out to her.

With a wry smile and a small laugh she took it, put it on. And for a while they sat there in silence.

Later, the helmet was again on the seat beside him, and she was trying to explain why it wasn't quite as simple as he made it sound. That you can't simply leave. "Even if I had someone to take over the store, I still have Grandmother and Aunt Edna."

He said, "They would survive your leaving. They have money enough. And they have Walter and Paul."

It was more complicated than that. She reminded him what the household was like. The well-guarded, non-threatening atmosphere controlled so carefully by the elderly ladies. "There would be no way to tell Grandmother I was going. It wouldn't be possible to tell her anything like that."

He knew what she meant. The Hayworth family never heard what they didn't want to hear. There had never been a conversation in that house on any subject not on the list of topics approved in advance as suitable for family discussion. To mention leaving would be as taboo as introducing a subject like sex, politics, or religion.

"Then just leave."

She said, "They would never accept the fact that I was gone."

He understood. They were silent for a moment.

He said, "I'm remembering a girl who was in the office to see me about a year ago. Almost two years ago. A girl named Lillian Crawford who had a problem something like yours."

He said, "She worked in a bakery. Sales clerk. And she came from a long line of people in which it was unprecedented for anyone to work, so her family thought her pretty strange."

He shook his head, and laughed. "I'm sure that for at least two generations back no girl in that family had either worked or married a man who did. And this poor kid, only twenty years old, had fallen in love with a cop., Twenty-two. He used to come to the bakery a lot, ostensibly to buy doughnuts, but mostly just to see her. He was crazy about her."

"And putting on weight." Faith laughed at her own joke.

He said, "I'm serious. Listen to this. He'd already arrested two of her brothers. One of them twice."

He said, "I'm not telling you this because the solution to her problem might be the same as yours. I'm just telling you what she did. All right?"

She said, "All right. So what happened."

He said, "At her house the only approved topics of conversation had to do with how impossible it was to find a job, how unfair the welfare people were, how unjust the courts were, and how all cops were pigs. And this girl knew there was no way to break into this kind of talk and say she was in love with a policeman. So what she and I together decided was that if she couldn't change the range of family conversation, she would at least neutralize it. Know what I mean?"

She didn't.

Cletus said, "She would come home from work and say, for example, that she had happened to meet a girl she had gone to school with who had just got back from California, where she'd worked for the telephone company in Sacramento. Had two kids, both red-haired. One with green eyes, one with blue. And so forth."

"Cletus, stop it. You're making this up and you know it."

He said, "Of course I'm not making this up. Would I lie to you?"

She said, "Of course you would." She said it in the flat positive tone of one who is certain she is right. But a moment later, "Go on and finish the story anyway."

He looked offended and for a moment she thought he wouldn't continue.

He did, finally. He said, "Anyway, it got so that they didn't pay any attention to anything she said. She told them once she'd met a bush pilot from Australia and might go back with him. He had an airplane with blue stripes down one side and red ones down the other. They told her that was nice and had she brought home any day-old doughnuts."

He said, "Day-old doughnuts can't be sold, you know. They're too dried out."

She hadn't known that. "What happened to the girl?"

"She came home the next day and told them she'd met a policeman who was going to buy a house in the country and a snowmobile and raise beagle hounds and maybe she'd marry him and quit work and just feed dogs every day."

"But not doughnuts," she said. "It's not good for their teeth."

He looked offended again. "I can see you're not really interested in this story."

She insisted she was. And please continue.

"That's about all there is to it. She married the cop and today they have a house in the country, one snowmobile, twin boys, and sixteen beagles."

She laughed so loud that people at the bar turned and looked at her. She said, "Cletus, you're crazy! You're absolutely crazy!" And she took a long sip of her wine, then sat looking at him and shaking her head. Cletus, her lovable but totally crazy brother!

He said, "Let's be serious."

She said, "All right. Let's be serious."

"There's something I often thought I'd tell you, but each time hesitated and changed my mind. Even now I am reluctant to tell it because I'm not sure how you'll react."

She asked, "Is it something that's true, or something you're going to make up?"

"It's true."

She sipped her wine, then said, more to herself than to him, "It was a waste of time to ask."

Cletus said, "The reason I mention it now, after all these years, is that possibly it explains why I found it easier to break away from the tight family pattern. Why I was able to feel more independent than you were, more an individual rather than simply one-sixth of the Hayworth family."

He paused, and she filled in the empty space with "Sounds interesting." She was being kind and giving him time to think. If he was making this up, he would need time to work it out as he went along.

"I hope you don't think I'm just making this up. Because if you will take my word that it really happened, it might help you see things from your own individual, unique, point of view. Which is basic to being free."

He looked very serious. Faith said, "You know I believe you. Please go ahead."

Then, just as he began, she interrupted him. "This sounds like a long story. Let me order another glass of wine first."

Cletus looked over to where the waitress was standing, caught her eye, and waved an arm. Then he continued.

"It's really a very small thing, actually, and perhaps I overestimated its importance."

Faith concentrated on trying to look serious and interested.

"Anyway, it was simply something I overheard one afternoon when I was about twelve years old. I remember it was late afternoon and I'd got home from swimming or playing baseball of something. Mother had had some friends in for bridge. They were in the living room. I had come in the back door very quietly because I didn't want to have to go in the front room and be introduced to all the dumb women."

He said, "I was in the kitchen fixing myself a sandwich. And making no noise at all."

The waitress came to the table. Cletus ordered another glass of wine for Faith and a beer for himself.

Then back to the story.

He said, "Mother's friends were talking about their families. One woman said she was sorry now that she had stopped with only one child. She wished that she'd had at least two. Maybe more. Another said she'd wanted only one but had ended up with three.

"Then I heard Mother say—and I remember it now as clearly as the day it happened—that she'd planned for only two but had ended up with four."

He paused and looked at her.

He had expected some reaction, but there seemed to be none. Not on the surface, at least. But she did look thoughtful.

"Later, when I thought about it, I was struck by what had not occurred to me before as being so unusual. That after Walter and Paul had been born there had been a gap of seven years before you and I came along. And the logic of it seemed clear enough. If Mother had planned to have four children she would have had them over nine or ten years at the most. And certainly not a gap of seven years between the second and third."

Faith didn't say anything. She quietly tapped her cigarette against the ashtray, tapped it long after there were any ashes to knock away.

He said, "Somehow, I felt a little less obligation to the family pattern after that. Which had nothing to do with whether or not I loved my father and mother—which I assure you I did—but it made it possible for me to love them in a different way. A better way, even. I didn't feel so obligated. I felt we were on the same level. That we had in common the fact that we are all the results of the chance happenings of fate." He said, "Who knows—or what difference does it make—whether Father and Mother were planned or just happened to come along? Or you and I? But somehow, for me, it put things in a slightly different perspective. I think that way back at age twelve I got the idea that we are all very separate organisms, and that we have to deal with life as we see it in our individual way."

He said, "Understand that I loved our parents as people. As parents. It was the pattern, the prescribed roles that we were all expected to play, that became less oppressing. Less unquestionable." He paused.

81

"But maybe that doesn't make any sense to you." And then he waited, insisting on some kind of response from her other than silence.

But there was still more silence from her for several moments. Until finally, "Cletus, you made that up and you know it."

He denied it. "Would I lie to you about something that serious?" And she said yes. "Yes, you would. You know very well you would." She said, "It's been years since I've been able to believe a thing you say. Even about something serious."

To show that his feelings had been hurt, he reached down and got his helmet and put it on his head.

The waitress came back with the drinks, and when she saw the helmet she thought for a moment she had come to the wrong booth. (Maybe even the wrong restaurant.) But Faith paid her, plus a nice tip, said it was all right. Faith tapped the side of her head with her index finger, looked briefly at Cletus, and back to the waitress.

The waitress understood. She got a lot of crazy people in here.

Before they parted that night, Faith asked him what she should tell Walter and Paul. Was he about ready to change his mind about the inheritance?

He told her he was satisfied with things the way they were.

He went with her to her car. She got in, rolled down the window, and before she drove away they talked a little longer.

He said, "There's something I want you to try for me."

She asked what.

"When you get home from work tomorrow, tell Grandmother Hayworth that you were delayed a few minutes because you'd met an old friend who is on his way to Peoria, Illinois, to take an executive position with the Peoria Pure Food Corporation."

She said, "Don't be silly."

He said, "Please. This is important to me."

She refused. "I won't do it. I couldn't even if I wanted to."

He said, "It would be hard. But you could do it if you tried."

"I don't intend to try."

But he seemed really disappointed. She relented a little. "Why would you suggest such a thing?"

He said, "It's something I'm working on. And it's something very important to me."

She swore softly. She loved her crazy brother and didn't want to hurt him. "It can't be that important."

He said, "Believe me, it is. I wouldn't ask you to do it if it weren't."

She sighed deeply. And thought a moment. "I don't think I can do it."

He looked hurt and disappointed.

"But if it is that important to you, then I'll try."

He said, "Please do it. Please."

Another deep sigh. "All right. I'll do it."

He looked elated. "Call me afterwards. I want to know your reaction. Not hers. Just yours."

She said, "Cletus, you're crazy."

"Maybe. Maybe I am. But please do what I asked. Okay?"

"Okay."

It had been a good evening. She was in no hurry to pull away. She said, "Take care of yourself."

"All right."

"The next time you see the young woman who married the policeman, tell her I sent my congratulations."

He said he'd tell her.

Chapter 11

Undoubtedly the turning point in the life of Cletus Hayworth was the afternoon Mrs. Bok gave him the file on Mary Kalinski.

She apologized for handing him this extra assignment because she was aware that already he had the biggest case load in the department, but he seemed to be the only one who had any spare time. Mrs. Bok ordinarily didn't give out compliments. She was simply giving honest recognition to the fact that Cletus was the worker whose clients seemed most often able to work out their problems. She valued this. It saved the state money.

An hour after she gave him the file he was waving it in front of her and threatening to sue her.

The life of Mary Kalinski had been rich in experiences not of her own choosing. She had been raped at the age of ten by her stepfather. Sent to reform school at fourteen. Pregnant at sixteen. Had her baby taken from her at seventeen.

She was eighteen before she could begin to fight back. And even that resulted in her being sent to a woman's correctional institution for six months.

At the age of eighteen, Mary Kalinski, five feet six inches, weighing only a hundred and ten pounds, in Farmington District Court had outwrestled a one-hundred-and-forty-five-pound police matron, thrown her to the floor, slipped from the grasp of a six-foot cop, pushed a probation officer across a row of seats, brushed past the elderly clerk of courts, and had got close enough to Judge Anthony Mazzero to strike one blow that knocked his honor's spectacles into a thousand fragments.

It was all in the file that Cletus was waving in the face of his startled supervisor.

He said, "For God's sake, have you read this!" He was loud and angry. He said, "Have you read this damn thing?"

She said of course she'd read it. "All I want you to do is to see the foster mother and arrange for the child to move easily from the foster home to its adoptive home. It won't take much work on your part."

The child she was referring to was the five-year-old child of Mary Kalinski.

He said, "I know what you're asking me to do. But did you hear what I asked *you*?"

She said, "Cletus, calm down. The child is five years old. He needs a permanent home. Security."

He repeated the question once more. "Did you hear what I asked you?"

She managed to remain calm. Her tone was conciliatory. "Cletus," she said, "if you don't want the case I'll assign it to someone else."

He said it was not a matter of who handled the case, and he banged the file on the desk. "The thing is that someone should be ashamed of himself."

Or herself, as the case was. The late Miss Bliss had been the worker. She had died a month ago and others were picking up parts of her case load as the need arose.

Mrs. Bok said, "I'd forgotten how you felt about adoptions. I should have remembered that we'd gone through this before." She reached out and took the file, placing it in front of her. "I'll give it to someone else."

Cletus reached out and returned the file to where it had been. In front of him. He opened it and he said, "Here is the story of a girl who had everything immoral,

85

illegal, and unjust done to her that could have been done."

He covered the highlights. There had been a string of bad foster homes, then reform school at fourteen. Home to a semialcoholic mother at fifteen. Pregnant at sixteen, by some college kid from New York or Boston who had worked at the summer resort where she had been employed as a waitress.

He said, "At sixteen, for God's sake. A waitress at sixteen!"

He turned back to the file. "After the baby was born she went to Boston to try to find the father and was caught trying to steal an apple or something and was held in jail, and the next day the welfare people claimed the baby had been abandoned, and took it from her."

He looked up at Mrs. Bok, who was leaning back in her chair, waiting for him to finish and leave the office. "Have you really read this or not?"

She said, "I told you I had. So why don't you just leave the file here and forget it. I'll assign it to someone else."

His response was to return once again to listing select incidents in society's extensive persecution of Mary Kalinski.

He said, "The judge gave her thirty days in the women's detention center for abandoning the baby and put her on six months probation. So after thirty days she got out, and as any decent person would do, went to where the child was and took it." He pushed through some loose pages in the file, looking for something, continuing to talk as he did so. "And when she was caught she was brought back to court and the judge gave her the six months to serve. And that was when she cleaned out the courtroom single-handedly."

He found the paper he was looking for.

"They asked her to sign a paper giving her baby up for adoption and she spit on it."

Cletus shook his head in admiration. "God damn! That's a real woman for you."

Mrs. Bok held out her hand. Her voice held a tone of quiet authority. "Cletus, give me the file."

He paid no attention. He went on, "While the mother was in jail, Miss Bliss asked the court for permission to have the child adopted without the mother's consent. Mary Kalinski heard about this. Heard the court had agreed to the adoption. But, actually, the baby *hadn't* been adopted because of a technicality. But Miss Bliss didn't tell Mary that. She let Mary continue to believe that it had been adopted. That was not right."

"Cletus, give me the file."

He said, softly, "I don't intend to do so."

He reminded her of the one thing about the case that could be considered amusing. That before the baby was even born, Mary had suspected that welfare might try to take it from her. So she named it Jeorge. With a J. So if it were taken and adopted she'd always be able to find it with a name like that.

The adoptive parents would, of course, have given the child a different name, but Mary hadn't thought of that.

"The irony," Cletus said, "is that when the papers were prepared for the court, someone typed the name wrong, spelled it George, with a G, and the papers bounced back because the name was different from the name on the certified birth certificate. And the papers weren't put through a second time until three months ago. And the court agreed to adoption without the mother's consent because the mother had made no effort to contact the child for four years."

He said, "Of course there had been no contact. The mother thought the child had been adopted. And no one here had the decency to try to locate her. As far as the record shows."

Mrs. Bok said, "It's no longer your case. I'm assigning it to someone else."

Cletus said, "If some worker puts this adoption through without trying to find the mother, I'll find the mother myself, help her bring suit against you, see that every newspaper in the country prints the story of how you let four years go by without making an effort to locate the mother and see if she was now able to care for her child."

The look Mrs. Bok gave him traveled on a direct beam of pure hate. She was too angry to speak. Her lips were tight together and her hands were doubled into fists.

Cletus took a letter from the file. Handwritten, four pages. "Here she tells Miss Bliss about how Jeorge is her boy and always will be and how she feels sorry for whoever goes through life thinking that because the name was changed, Jeorge is now theirs. And she thanks this department for being so kind as to take Jeorge from her while she was in jail and unable to defend herself."

He folded the letter and put it in his pocket. "I plan to keep this because I might want to make some copies for the press."

He took the file and stood up.

"There is one little fact that will make you look bad when Mary Kalinski sues you for a million dollars. And that is the fact that she wouldn't have been hard to find." He said, "You know why?"

There was no change in the expression on Mrs. Bok's face. Her lips stayed one long thin line.

Cletus said, "All you would have had to do was to check the telephone book. It's right there. Mary Kalinski. Grove Street. Right here in Farmington." And he walked out.

He tried to reach Mary Kalinski by phone that afternoon and throughout the evening, but there was no answer.

He was living at that time in a small top floor apartment in one of the poorer sections of Farmington. Peeling paint, bare floors, furniture salvaged from the Goodwill. But comfortable. A girl from the first floor apartment, Sue Bunnell, student at a hairdressing school, not too bright but good humored, soft shaped, and very en-

88

joyable in bed, was spending the night with him, as she did from time to time.

Just before midnight he tried one last time to reach Mary Kalinski by phone. He got out of bed and dialed the number.

Sue asked petulantly, "Why do you keep jumping out of bed? Now come on back here and stay."

She patted the exact spot on the bed where she wanted him to return to. Near where she was, so she could press her heavy breasts flat against his bare chest. She spread out on the bed to show how much she would welcome his quick return. "Now c'mon back."

He said, "I got to keep trying to reach this person. I told you that."

She moved her naked body around and complained some more. She said, "I wish I knew who's so important you got to reach them this time of night."

And he said, "I told you. I'm trying to reach a client."

She reached down, angry, jerked the blankets up. She said, "Yeh, I bet!"

And turned her back to him.

He let it ring a long time. There was still no answer.

Chapter 12

The next morning Cletus had a few words with the adoption worker, Julia Kauffman. She was waiting at his desk when he reported for work. She was dark haired, slender, a graduate of Smith College, and belligerently humane. She loved children. She wanted them all to have good homes where they could find warm love and real security. Julia herself had not had warm love and real security, and probably could not have named more than three people she had even known who had. But that, to her, was what waited at the end of the adoption process for every homeless child. She could not easily be kind to anyone who would deprive a parentless child of a real home.

And she saw Cletus as just such a person, according to what she had learned from Mrs. Bok.

"This child," she said to Cletus, in a low hard voice, "must be adopted. He must not be bounced from foster home to foster home for the rest of his life."

She did not take the seat Cletus offered her but stood at the side of the desk looking down at him.

"I didn't have in mind bouncing the kid about," Cletus said, "like he were a rubber ball. I had in mind returning him to his mother."

"Then that should have happened long ago. Not at the last minute before I place him with an ideal couple waiting to give him the love and security of a good home."

"Far as I know," Cletus said, "he has a good home. I just got the case yesterday."

"He had no real security."

Cletus thought about that for a moment, and had to agree. Anyone who can be given to someone else without having anything to say about it is not very secure. He said, "That's true."

"These people will give him their name."

"What if he doesn't like it?" And after a moment, "What is the name, incidentally?"

She didn't want to say and he had the idea it might be a funny name.

He said, "Nothing wrong with Kalinski."

Miss Kauffman had run into this type of problem before.

She leveled with him. She told him to his face that she had encountered his type before. "Your kind of social worker can never let go a case. You are the typical anal personality. You can't let go."

Anal types are the result of over-severe toilet training. Cletus knew that much.

He said, "I don't remember. That was too long ago." And while she was digging through her handbag for some pictures to show him he tried to remember the details of those early toilet training years.

She had snapshots of the couple who wanted to adopt the boy. They looked like a nice clean couple in their late twenties. The man was sturdy, stocky, had a crew cut. She was rather plain, wore a simple print dress. Miss Kauffman showed him two pictures first. One taken by the husband of his wife standing stiffly by the outdoor grill in the backyard, and one by her of him standly stiffly by the outdoor grill in the backyard.

He was an engineer. She was a secretary for an insurance company. Miss Kauffman said, "She is going to give up her job as soon as Jeorge is really theirs."

They were no doubt active in church affairs, were good citizens, voted against radicals, bathed regularly. The inside of their house, as other pictures showed, was com-

91

plete with fresh new furniture just waiting for a little boy to not put his feet on it.

Cletus said, "Are these the kind of people who should be given a child whose mother single-handedly cleaned out a courtroom to try to keep him?"

He handed the snapshots back to her.

She said, "The husband is a college graduate and successful. Jeorge should have parents who will put him through college."

"Maybe he won't want to go."

She said, "Jeorge is not an ordinary boy. He has an IQ of a hundred and forty."

"Then he probably won't want to go."

She told him she was taking Jeorge tomorrow for a weekend visit with the prospective adoptive parents. If things went well, he would go the following week to stay for good.

"Tell them," Cletus said, "they will be sued by the mother for a million dollars. The mother will sue this department and the adoptive parents."

He added, "I will help her do it."

She threw her handbag over her shoulder and left in anger to find Mrs. Bok.

Cletus left, in happy anticipation, to find Mary Kalinski and tell her that her child had not been adopted after all, and she could have him back.

The address listed in the phone book for Mary Kalinski was a three-story, six-apartment building in a section of town that was a bit run down, but not the worst. There were fewer junked cars in the backyards here than in some places, and the streets had been paved within the last ten years and some sections of sidewalk were still intact. The house was gray, more from years than from paint, but the yard was clean and there was grass in spots.

The Kalinski apartment was on the third floor. He knocked a number of times, but no one answered.

Finally the door across the hall opened and a woman, a small, plump, grandmotherly type, opened the door.

He asked, "Does Mary Kalinski live here?"

She said, "Yes, but she's not at home."

"Is she working?"

"No."

"Oh. Do you know where she is?"

The woman seemed to be enjoying this guessing game. She nodded her head, yes.

For God's sake! But gently, "Where is she please?"

"She's gone to Vermont."

"Do you know when she'll be back?" Then he hastily rephrased the question. "When will she be back?"

The woman said, "She'll be back tonight. Very late, she said. After midnight. She's gone to her mother's funeral."

She asked Cletus why he was looking for her.

He told her he was an investigator for a firm where she'd applied for a job. He said, "I have to check out her references, talk with her neighbors, that kind of thing."

He tried to remember some of the other names on the mailboxes downstairs. "You Mrs. Snyder?"

She said, "No. Mrs. Taikowski."

He said, "Of course. How stupid of me. May I come in?"

The door opened into her kitchen. The aroma of fresh baked bread filled the room. It smelled good and he told her so. That pleased her.

"I like the colors in your kitchen," he said. "I have the same colors in mine except that your gray has a little more life to it."

That pleased her.

"Very good taste."

"Thank you."

They exchanged smiles.

"I used to know a Taikowski family in Cranesville," he said. "Fine people, the Taikowski family. Girls as pretty

93

as any you ever laid eyes on. You aren't by any chance from that area are you?"

She wasn't. She was from Hartsdale. Her maiden name had been Plew. She spelled it for him.

He said he had passed through Hartsdale many times. Beautiful place. Didn't know anyone there, but he had gone to college with a fellow named Plew who was studying to be a doctor. Brilliant chap. From somewhere in that general area.

Then he asked, "Do you mind telling me something about your neighbor, Mary Kalinski?"

She was glad to.

He came out with the name of the firm Mary worked for, the church she attended, and the name of the family doctor she went to for her back problem. (Wrestling hundred-and-fifty-pound police matrons around would leave anyone with a back problem.) She didn't have men in her apartment, Mrs. Taikowski said. At least not overnight. Didn't drink or stay out all night. (She amended that a little. Well, she did drink some. But not to excess.) Worked steady. Never caused any trouble in the building. Everyone liked her.

"And she'll be back tonight?"

"That's what she told me before she left. Very late. Said she was taking tomorrow off."

"So she'll be home tomorrow."

"I suppose so."

He said, "Thank you very much."

A few blocks away there was a phone booth on the corner and he placed some calls.

The priest at Saint Joseph's said he didn't know Mary Kalinski very well. He had transferred to this parish only four months ago. But he knew she attended church every Sunday. No, he hadn't heard any gossip or scandal about her. Yes, as far as he knew she was a person of good moral character. But he had talked to her only a few times.

Her doctor, reluctant at first, ended by giving a good recommendation. The back problem wasn't enough to keep her from working, certainly. He hadn't seen her recently, now that her back condition was so much better. No, he knew of no scandal or gossip about her. Rather liked her, himself. Cheerful, usually. Good disposition. Yes, he understood that she'd had a lot of problems when she was younger. But sómetimes people do change, he said.

The young woman in the personnel office where Mary Kalinski worked supplied the information that Mary had a good work record, had never caused any trouble, was well liked by her fellow workers. She had been there nearly two years. Her last rating by the supervisor had been excellent.

No, she wasn't working today because she'd gone to Vermont for her mother's funeral. Wouldn't be back until Monday.

Gossip or scandal? No. Not since she'd been here, anyway.

He was back to the office before the end of the day and in to see Mrs. Bok.

He said, "I strongly suggest you not to go through with the adoption. I checked her out carefully and she's clean. She could have people in court tomorrow testifying that she's of sound moral character, a steady worker, and a good citizen. I talked with her minister, doctor, employer. And neighbors. The woman right across the hall, even. Who had only good things to say about her. In fact," he said, "you'd think she was some kind of damn saint or something."

"Does she want the child back?" Mrs. Bok asked. "I mean, *really* want it?"

Cletus said, "Christ!" and put his head in his hands for a moment.

"I swear I still think you never read the record. You couldn't have!"

He said, "We're talking about a girl who wiped out a courtroom full of police officers, knocked the judge off the bench. And you ask if she wants the kid back!"

He did dramatic things like hit his fist against the side of his head. Put both hands over his face. Lifted his eyes toward heaven and groaned.

She said, "All right. Don't carry on."

Cletus said, "All these years the taxpayers have supported this child in a foster home just because you and Miss Bliss didn't look in the phone book and get the girl's address and find if she was now able to care for her child herself." He added, "That, too, would probably be brought out in court."

She said, "Look, Cletus, I'll go along with you, although I'm not at all sure you're right. But I have to trust your judgment. You're a good worker, maybe the only good worker in the whole office. So I'll do it."

"We've got to do it. To keep the newspapers from getting hold of the story."

"How soon can she take the boy?"

He said, "It's got to be tomorrow. If not, Julia Kauffman, the girl from the adoption division, will place it with the adoptive parents, and then it will be too late."

Mrs. Bok muttered something under her breath. And made a few dramatic gestures of her own. "All right. Discharge the child to his mother tomorrow. And I'll deal with the adoption division."

Then she added, in the most ominous tone she could manage, "But by God, Cletus, if anything goes wrong, I swear I'll fire you on the spot. And I'll see you don't ever get a job again anywhere. Ever!"

And that goes for all long-haired kids everywhere.

He said, "Trust me. Nothing will go wrong."

He called the foster mother, Mrs. Alice Basil, and told her of the change in plans. He asked her to have the boy ready to return to his mother in the morning. Before noon.

He said, "I know it's short notice."

She said, "It certainly is!" And she didn't sound happy about the change. "Miss Kauffman was going to pick him up tomorrow afternoon for a weekend visit to his new home."

Cletus said, "I know. But we located his real mother just today."

Chapter 13

Because Mary Kalinski was not expected back until after midnight, Cletus waited until ten o'clock in the morning to call her. He wanted her to get as much sleep as she could. Even so, the voice that answered the phone sounded very tired.

She said, "Yes, this is Mary Kalinski."

He said, "I'm sorry to wake you."

The sleepy sounding voice said, "That's all right."

"I wanted to make sure you'd got back from Vermont."

She said, "Yes, I got back."

"Sorry to hear about your mother dying. That's too bad."

"Thank you. Who's this?"

He said, "This is Cletus Hayworth. I want to stop around later this morning. Are you going to be home?"

"I suppose so. What do you want?"

He said, "I'll tell you when I get there."

"I don't want to buy anything."

Cletus said, "I'm not selling anything. But I've something very important to see you about. And I don't want to discuss it on the phone."

She protested. He insisted. She finally agreed. "But not before noon. I've got to get some sleep. I didn't get back until two in the morning."

He said, "It will be noon before I can get there. I've got to go to Coltsville to pick up someone first."

Coltsville was where Mrs. Basil lived. And Jeorge.

"Try to be up and dressed. I've got something for you that will make you very happy."

The scene as it ran through his mind was that she would open the door and he would introduce himself and say that he and his young friend—and he would look down at the little boy—had come to see her. And she would say that that was nice, and what a handsome young lad. And Cletus would say, yes, he really is a fine little boy. Happy, intelligent, healthy, good-looking boy. And she would say to the boy, what is your name, and the boy would say Jeorge. Spelled with a J. And within seconds everyone would be happy and laughing and hugging one another and it would probably be one of the moments Cletus would remember all his life.

She muttered something and hung up.

He hung up, too, and headed for Mrs. Basil's house.

Mrs. Basil, cheeks red splotched and eyes swollen, had cried all night. She planned to resume as soon as the child and his social worker were out of sight.

She had known all along that the day would come when he would be taken from her, but it wasn't something you can prepare yourself for. She had loved him so much. To her he was more than all the money in the world.

Mrs. Basil was a widow. Her children were grown. Jeorge had been her whole world, and without him life would not be worth living.

Her whole world was standing stiff and straight in the center of the living room. Mrs. Basil gestured toward him and said in a flat voice, "That's Jeorge. Jeorge, this is Mr. Hayworth."

She motioned toward two suitcases and three boxes just inside the door. "These are his things."

Jeorge was handsome, slender, a clean and shining face, light blond hair neatly trimmed and parted on one side. On his face was a small stoic smile. He was flawlessly dressed, a clean white shirt and a small bow tie, pressed trousers and polished black shoes. His right arm hung somewhat relaxed at his side. The other was bent up across his chest and the hand grasped a small white prayer book. Only his eyes moved as Cletus approached.

Cletus bent down and the two of them shook hands rather formally.

Mrs. Basil said, "I didn't tell him anything except that you were coming for him."

Cletus said, "All right." Then to the boy. "Will you come with me? It's all right."

The boy's lips tightened a bit, but he nodded. Yes, he would come.

"Good."

While Cletus loaded the boy's things in the car, Mrs. Basil huddled with the boy off to one side, giving him last-minute instruction in the manner of an impassioned football coach giving his quarterback specific details on how to run the next three plays in the final thirty-two seconds of the big game.

Then there were the final hugs, tears, and good-byes.

In the car the boy sat up straight, still clutching the prayer book, gave one last wave to his foster mother and home and held it like a long salute until they had turned the corner at the end of the block. The boy didn't look back. He didn't speak. And, as Cletus didn't have much to say, the trip was made in almost total silence.

On the way Cletus changed his mind about how to handle the presentation of child to mother. The earlier plan was too risky. He would go to the door by himself, let her get over her hysterical thanks and embraces and tears. He would then go to the car and bring Jeorge in.

So he went alone to the third-floor apartment and knocked. He had to knock a number of times before there was an answer. Across the hall he could hear sounds from Mrs. Taikowski's kitchen. Finally the door to the Kalinski apartment opened partway and a woman looked sleepily out at him. Her eyelids drooped wearily. Her hair was uncombed, and one hand clutched an old robe wrapped about her. She was about fifty years old.

He asked, "Is Mary Kalinski in, please?"

She took time to wake up a bit more before answering. She said, "I'm Mary Kalinski."

They looked silently at each other for several long moments.

He said, "I'm looking for the Mary Kalinski who's about twenty-two years old."

She blinked her eyes slowly, smiled the soft smile of one who doesn't mind having been awakened because it was going to feel so good to be able to go back to bed and to sleep again. She said, "You must mean my daughter. Her name is Mary, too." She added, "She'd be twenty-two."

His face brightened a bit. "That's right. Is she in?"

The woman shook her head. No.

"No?" He paused a moment before asking, "Do you know when she'll be back?"

That got only another sleepy smile and a shake of the head. So he asked, "She does live here, doesn't she?" And the answer was that she kept shaking her head and smiling.

Half a dozen seconds passed and they only looked at each other.

"Do you know where she is?"

She reached up to brush some hair from her eyes, her other hand clutching at the robe to keep it from falling open. "No."

She said, "I haven't seen her for two years. Or more."

She answered his next question even before he asked it. She said, "I'm sorry. I'm afraid I haven't the least idea where she is."

The smile of her face slowly gave way to a look of concern, because the young man just stood there, not asking

101

more questions, just looking at her. She asked, "Is anything wrong?"

She thought he looked pale.

He said, "Wrong?" And blinked his eyes and looked at her. And after a moment managed a smile. That was followed by a very brief and unenthusiastic laugh. "No," he said, "except that I'm sorry I woke you up."

He raised his hand in a small gesture of farewell and turned to leave. But after only two or three steps he stopped, turned, said, "I'll come back another day and talk to you." And he waved again and was gone.

She watched him leave. He seemed a little unsteady on the stairs and she waited until she heard the front door downstairs close.

He hadn't looked as if he had been drinking. But then, he might have been.

She hoped he'd be all right.

She shrugged her shoulders, made her way back to bed, and within five minutes was asleep again.

Jeorge Henry Kalinski, less than two hours away from his home and mother in Coltsville, found himself in a new kind of world. Mr. Hayworth had called it Sandy's. Jeorge had a large glass of Coke in front of him and a bag of potato chips. Across the room some people were sitting on tall stools and eating and drinking. There was laughing and once he heard someone swear. He had never been in a place like this before, but something about the sounds and smell made him feel relaxed and not unhappy.

Mr. Hayworth was making a phone call. He had made several phone calls. Now he returned to the booth and they looked at each other.

Cletus said, "How would you like to take off your tie? It makes you look uncomfortable." Without waiting for an answer, he reached over and unhooked it. "That better?"

It had not been uncomfortable, really, but Jeorge said, "Yes sir."

"And you don't need to call me sir. All right?"

Jeorge said, "All right."

There was loud conversation from where the men were sitting on stools and some words were used that Mrs. Basil would have been shocked at. Jeorge looked up to see if Mr. Hayworth was shocked. He didn't seem to be. He didn't even seem to have noticed.

"You got other clothes, haven't you, besides that suit and white shirt you got on? You got sweaters, sport shirts, that kind of thing?"

Jeorge said, "Sure, I got lots of clothes." He could tell Mr. Hayworth didn't like coats and white shirts.

He watched Mr. Hayworth finish his second bottle of beer.

"Want another Coke?"

His glass was still half full. Jeorge said, "No, thank you."

"Would you like a hamburger?"

A hamburger would be good. "Yes, please."

"More potato chips?"

"No, thank you."

He watched Mr. Hayworth slide out of the booth once more, saying, "I'll ask the waitress to get us a couple hamburgers."

In a short time he was back, with another bottle of beer. And he lit another cigarette. That was something Jeorge hadn't seen very often before. No one around Mrs. Basil's house had smoked.

"Look," Cletus said, "I'll tell you what we're gonna do." He sipped his beer and thought for a moment. "First, we're going to look through your suitcases and see what kind of clothes you got. You must have something besides white shirts and bow ties." He took a deep drink of the beer. "We'll see what kind of clothes you need. You know, things to play in. And go out and buy them."

"All right."

The waitress set a hamburger in front of each of them.

"You got a ball glove?"

The boy shook his head.

"We'll get you a ball glove."

He said, "I called the office and said I wouldn't be back today, so we got time to do anything we want. We'll buy you a ball glove, get you some new clothes, maybe go to a movie. Cowboy show or something. And for dinner we'll go out to a place I know called Burger Heaven. You'll like that."

Then he looked at the boy again. He said, "You got a fishing pole?"

And when the boy shook his head, Cletus said, "We'll get you one of those, too."

The waitress finised making out the bill and dropped it in front of Cletus. She looked down, smiling at the boy. She was a friendly young woman. It made her happy to see a man and boy be such good friends. This was the way it should be.

She said to the lad, "Hey, your father's being pretty good to you, isn't he?"

She patted Jeorge on the head, smiled at Cletus, and left.

Jeorge sat there with the hamburger poised half an inch from his lips, eyes big, looking across the table. He lowered the sandwich a few inches and looked at Cletus. On his face was the look of a child who had been lost in the deep woods for seven days and now thought for the first time that maybe he recognized a familiar landmark. But couldn't quite believe it.

He said, "Are you really my father?"

He was sure the answer was no. Mrs. Basil had told him that he didn't have a father.

Cletus returned the look. Straight. Eye to eye.

What else can you do when the kid's only five. Almost six. And has been lost in the woods for seven days.

He said, "Of course."

This couldn't be true. Jeorge looked at the tall man with the mustache that dipped down at the ends. The friendly man with the dark curly hair soft smile. He cocked his head a bit to one side and asked, skeptically, afraid to believe, "Really?" He said, "Are you really my father?"

Cletus said, "Would I lie to you?"

The boy knew of course not! He'd been told enough times what happened to people who told lies. He smiled and raised the hamburger to his mouth and took a big bite.

Mrs. Basil had been wrong. He had a father after all. He felt very happy.

Chapter 14

Dr. Eugene Barber concluded, finally, that he'd had all he could take of Cletus Hayworth and his problems.

Psychiatrists, too, have problems. And Dr. Barber had his. Not the kind you might project onto your patients, of course, unless they, too, happened to have recently bought a house that had been overpriced to begin with and was now going to cost a small fortune to make even livable. This bit of unpleasantness crouched in the back of his mind, ready to spring into consciousness at any opportunity. Such as a patient talking at great length on a matter of no significance. Or, as Mr. Hayworth always did, to elaborate at length on matters of pure fabrication. It is hard to concentrate on what the patient is saying if you know it is irrelevant. And to let the mind wander for even a brief moment is to have your tranquillity ripped apart by thoughts of leaking roofs, wet basements, house supports shot through with damp rot and termites.

The last time Hayworth had been here he had spent most of the fifty minutes describing in detail a dream he'd had in which his psychiatrist had been a Christlike figure, bestowing blessings upon all, making cures like crazy, but ultimately being driven from the field by his professional colleagues because he hadn't charged for his services. And for curing too many people too quickly. Admittedly, it had been amusing, being a dream representing a basic hostility toward his therapist. But after a while such fantasies become tiresome.

And today his patient was fabricating a long and tiresome story about having somehow acquired a small child that didn't belong to him. Or to anyone else, apparently.

Dr. Barber had been seeing this young man now for more than a year, twice a month, with no appreciable results. He was ready to give up. Enough was enough.

But Dr. Barber had to get through the remainder of this hour by some means.

"You say that this five-year-old boy lives with you and thinks you're his father?"

He cleared his throat and added, "That's very interesting."

Cletus said, "Yes. A waitress said something that made the boy think I was his father and I didn't have the heart to tell him I wasn't."

"I can understand that. How could one possibly tell a small child you aren't his father."

Cletus said, "Right! Especially when the kid looks like he's been lost in the forest for seven days."

Barber agreed. "Seven days is a long time."

"It is for a child only five years old. Almost six."

To himself, Barber said, This is an insult to my profession. Aloud, mechanically, he said, "Tell me more about it."

In his mind he began to draft a letter to Walter Hayworth in which he would include his final prognosis and would submit his last bill. He would say that he could not in good conscience certify that the young man was capable of spending his inheritance intelligently. Neither now nor in the foreseeable future.

Against his will his mind formed a picture of water seeping through cracks in the basement floor. Although the contractor claimed that sealing the cracks would not solve the problem, he wondered if it might not be worth a try anyway. A new drainage system would cost more than he could afford at this time.

"I'm sorry, but I missed what you said about the boy's name."

Cletus repeated, "Jeorge Henry Kalinski. Jeorge

spelled with a J. I said that that was because the mother suspected welfare would try to take the child from her, and she thought that if she named him Jeorge, with a J, she would always be able to find him."

Barber said, "That was clever."

Cletus said, "I think so, too."

Buying the house had been a mistake. And all because his wife had been overimpressed by the fact that the famous psychiatrist and writer Dr. Paul Paulson lived just up the road. His wife had got caught up with the idea that if they lived there they would automatically become part of an elite crowd of psychiatrists, writers, and other famous people.

"The boy would have been adopted without the mother's consent," Cletus said, "except that the worker who'd had the case died and my supervisor asked me to help get the child out of the foster home and into the adoptive home. But when I saw that no effort had been made to locate the mother, I refused to go along with the plan. Then I thought I had found the mother but discovered that I'd located the grandmother instead."

"A natural mistake," Barber said. "Could have happened to anyone."

"They both have the same name," Cletus said. And added, "You're the only one I've told this to. I would be in real trouble if my office ever found out what happened."

Barber said, "Yes, that's true." He tried to push the house from his mind. He tried to concentrate on what his patient was saying. "And what do you plan to do now?"

"Find the mother."

"That seems sensible," Barber said. "And who's going to take care of the child?"

Cletus said, "There's this girl who lives in my apartment building who goes to hairdressing school. Her younger sister is visiting her. The younger sister cares for the boy during the day. She thinks the boy is my nephew.

But I'm moving next week to Fairlawn Estates, to a furnished apartment where no one knows me. There's a private day care center there where I can leave the boy while I'm working."

Dr. Barber was pretty certain it had been his wife's idea more than his that they buy the house. He recalled certain questions he had raised regarding the wisdom of buying an old house. Not that this freed him from all responsibility. Even though it had been his wife's overreaction to the fact that Paulson lived only three houses up the road that had blinded them to the house's obvious defects. And the irony of it all was that Paulson lived most of the year in his New York City apartment, spent very little time in his country home, and tended to avoid his neighbors even when he was up here. The dreams of a fascinating social life with intellectuals and artists had faded and the house's structural defects had remained.

"He's a very good-looking little boy," Cletus said, "and has a high IQ."

Barber said, "Fascinating," and again tried to immerse himself in what his patient was saying. He asked, "Is the boy in school?"

"No, but he has to be by September. But by then I will have found the mother. If I haven't, I'll move from the area and keep the kid with me."

"That would be interesting."

Cletus said, "I don't know how interesting it would be, but I have no choice. I'm responsible for getting the boy into this mess, so I've got to get him out of it." He added, "I strongly believe in family responsibility."

"Look," Barber said, forcing himself to focus on the subject at hand, like a truck driver at night striving to fight off sleep, "what kind of feeling do you get when you think about this child? How does all this relate to your own childhood?"

Cletus didn't understand.

"What I mean," Barber said, "is how do you feel about this boy's relationship to you? For instance, he didn't have a father until you came along, did he?"

Cletus said, "He used to have a foster father, but he died."

"But not a real father? One who loved him?"

Cletus didn't know about that. Maybe the foster father had really loved him. And the foster mother, too. She was heartbroken because the boy had been moved. Of course, they had given the boy a lot of stupid ideas, but that's what happens to most kids.

Barber tried another approach. He said, "You did say that you rescued the boy from adoption. I distinctly recall your use of the word rescued. You *rescued* the boy. Now, does this arouse any feelings in you about what you wish might have happened to you?" He said, "Do you see any relationship between this boy and you that is similar to or different from the relationship between you and your own father?"

Cletus said, "I didn't want to be rescued from my father. I loved my father."

Barber said, "You used the word responsible. Now, what is your first reaction to that word as it applies to the father-child relationship?"

Cletus said, "I think people are responsible for their actions. Because of me, this boy lost his foster home, plus his chance of being adopted. So now I'm responsible for him." He added, "Only, of course, until I find his mother."

Dr. Barber gave up. He leaned back, sighed, and tried not to hear anything said by the young man on the couch.

He worked out some figures on the pad in front of him. He could sell the house now at five thousand less than he had paid for it, or put five thousand into it and sell it for the same price he had paid for it. Or there was always the outside chance that he could find someone who would buy the house without taking time to investigate carefully.

After all, Paul Paulson did live only a few houses away.

Fragments of his patient's fantasy broke through to his consciousness. "I have some leads to follow. Besides, when the mother hears I'm looking for her, she'll assume it is about her child and she'll get in touch with me."

Perhaps if he only painted the house and put on a new roof. For under a thousand.

He said, "That's still a lot of money."

Cletus said, "Beg pardon?"

Barber corrected himself. "What I meant was that that's a long chance. A big gamble. But it might work."

Then their time was up. He said, "Mr. Hayworth, I'm not going to make another appointment for you. I believe I have done all I can for you, and shall write to your brother Walter accordingly." He added, "I assume this is satisfactory with you."

It wasn't at all. Cletus suddenly felt rejected and insecure. Right now, when he was in trouble, he could have used some advice and support. But the tone of the doctor's voice made it clear that the decision was final.

But he was slow in getting off the couch.

Dr. Barber cleared his throat impatiently. He said, "You can go now."

So he forced himself to his feet, reluctantly. For the first time he was aware how good it had been to have someone to talk to about his problems. That he would no longer have the opportunity to do so left him with a feeling of depression.

He put on his helmet.

Then Dr. Barber permitted himself one last and quite unprofessional comment.

111

Unprofessional, but surely forgivable. After all, psychiatrists are only human.

He said, "You can go now . . . And take your little boy with you."

Chapter 15

Mrs. Mary Kalinski was forty-nine years old. Three times married, twice divorced. Now separated from her third husband, who had also been her first husband, Michael Kalinski.

Mother of six, she had fed children to the world like quarters to a slot machine.

A brief, colorful spin for the money, then nothing.

One killed in a war, one in an auto accident. Steve, the second oldest, in jail. Paula with her three the nearest to a payoff, and that not more than a letter every few weeks and cards at Christmas and her birthday. Sonya overseas with her husband in Germany. And now a young man looking for Mary.

She showed him a photograph taken at least four years ago. He asked if he could have it and she said it was one of only a few she had left. He said he'd return it, but she knew he wouldn't.

"You haven't told me why you're looking for her."

He said, "I'm sorry. I thought I had." He examined the snapshot closely. "You don't have anything that shows more of the face?"

Maybe there was one somewhere. But she shook her head.

"Are you from the police?"

"No, but that is close." And he smiled. "Actually, I'm doing some amateur detective work for an old friend. He was in love with your daughter some years ago. He'd prefer that I not mention his name. He didn't meet Mary until after he was already married. Now he's divorced. He has become rather well known, I would say. And well off. He wrote and asked me if I'd find Mary and let him know if she is married. If she isn't, he'd like to write to her."

She was skeptical. "Is that really why you're looking for her?"

He said, "Would I lie to you?"

He did look honest. But Mary was forty-nine years old. She said, "You would if you wanted to."

She watched him put the picture carefully into his wallet.

He looked tired. She sensed that he shouldered a heavy burden of some kind. Beneath the carefree and youthful exterior she thought she saw a worried and troubled mind. And though she hesitated to discourage him even further, she felt she had to warn him. She said, "You will have trouble finding her."

He said, "I suppose so. But I've got to try. For my friend's sake."

She told him, "She doesn't use her real name any more. At least, that's what I heard."

She saw his shoulders slump even lower, and heard him mutter something under his breath.

"Do you know what name she uses?"

"No."

He thought about that for a moment. It's not that easy to just change your name. You have to do it through probate court. There would be a record. He mentioned these thoughts aloud.

She said, "I suppose she uses her real name for social security and taxes and things like that. But that's all."

She was probably right. It could be done.

He asked why she had changed her name.

Mrs. Kalinski admitted it had been her fault. "She was mad at something I did. Something I realize now was

114

dumb. Something that hurt her very much. She stormed out of the house, angry, said she wasn't ever coming back. That she didn't any longer even consider herself a Kalinski and had no intention of ever using that name again."

Cletus asked how long ago that had been. She said well over a year. "Closer to two, probably."

Then she asked, "Why don't you put an advertisement in the paper?"

He thought, God! That would do it.

To his mind came the horrible image of Mrs. Bok waving the advertisement in his face and asking him to explain why he had discharged the child to its mother without knowing where the mother was.

And what would be the charge for having a small boy in your possession who didn't belong to you?

Kidnapping, maybe?

"I don't want to do that," he said. "I just want you to tell her friends that it's important I find her."

She said, "All right."

"Do you know anyone who might know where she is?"

She said she could think of several people who might know.

"I'll check in a day or two. If you get any leads let me know and I'll follow up on them."

She said, "Don't call me at work."

He promised not to.

He left her his name and phone number and made her promise to call him if she learned how he could find her daughter.

He moved from his apartment on Center Street.

Jeorge asked if he should keep telling people he was Cletus's nephew and Cletus said no.

"Jeorge Hayworth?"

Cletus said, "What else?" Then changed his mind. "Except that I never did really like that Jeorge with a J bit. Why don't I call you Hank, from your middle name, Henry."

The kid liked that. So from then on it was Hank.

Sometimes Cletus would wake up in the middle of the night and groan.

During the day he kept up the search.

He moved to Fairlawn Estates at the very southern edge of town, almost to the Glenbrook line. Fairlawn Estates was a garden apartment complex, which didn't mean that anyone had a garden, only that there was grass beside the three long rows of small apartments occupied mostly by newlyweds, single persons, and older couples whose children had grown and gone. It was expensive, and not the kind of place Cletus would have chosen for a pad.

But things worked out well. He found a nice grandmotherly sort of woman, a Mrs. Gogle, who was willing to baby-sit at any hour. And there was a private day care program nearby run by two young women on vacation from college. They didn't require dumb things like birth certificates or doctor's examinations. Hank attended their program from eight-thirty in the morning until three-thirty in the afternoon. Mrs. Gogle then took over until Cletus got home.

Then came the first signs of trouble, and from a direction he had not anticipated.

Mrs. Basil phoned two days after he'd moved the boy to say that Jeorge had left some clothes behind and she'd drop them off to the boy if Cletus would tell her where Jeorge and his mother lived. But Cletus stopped by her house and picked up the clothes. He said he'd deliver them for her. A little later she called to say she had a gift for Jeorge, something she had ordered for him before he had left. And Cletus said he would pick it up. She said no, she wanted to give it to him herself. Cletus refused to permit it. He said it was still too early for her to visit the child. It would hamper his adjustment to his new home.

That explanation didn't satisfy her. She spoke sharply with him, criticizing him for the way the move had been handled in the first place.

He got a little sharp with her in return.

She said she was going to see the boy and he had better accept that. He said she wasn't going to do so. And not to bother him about it again.

She said she supposed she'd have to talk to Mrs. Bok about it.

He checked discreetly with welfare. No record in recent years of Mary Kalinski. Probate court had no record of a Mary Kalinski changing her name. That was somehow encouraging. He tried the social security office, but they didn't permit the use of their records for locating people except in very unusual circumstances, and then only at the request of the police, state, or federal organizations.

At the state employment office there was a record for Mary Kalinski, but the last entry was a year old. They had got her a job at a small diner in the Four Corners shopping center. Not a very good place to work, they admitted. Low wages, not very good tips. They had not been surprised to hear that she'd left after a few months.

Unfortunately, the man at the employment office who had known Mary best, the one who had helped her get jobs over the years, had died about three months ago. If he were still around, he would have known where the girl was, probably. No one else in the office had known Mary very well.

He talked to the manager of the diner where Mary had worked. The man said he remembered her. Nice kid. Good worker. Everyone had liked her. Young and pretty. Very independent. Quit without saying where she was going or what she was going to do. Simply called one day and said she wouldn't be coming in again. They'd often wondered what had happened to her.

Was he from the police?

No. A cousin from out of town. Hadn't seen her for years. Thought he'd look her up.

Someone suggested he try the new Women's Center, which offered help to women looking for employment. So he went there.

The Women's Center was in an old two-story house in what had once been a choice residential neighborhood on a hill overlooking the downtown business section. The neighborhood had deteriorated rapidly in recent years and the house had kept pace. In faded gray with peeling white trim, it seemed to sink dejectedly behind the high untrimmed hedge that surrounded the building. Inside, space had been provided for programs dealing with women's activities. Here you could get help or informa- tion on such matters as employment, sex counseling, abortion, birth control, welfare rights, and women's liberation.

A thin, rather shy young woman, brown hair, rimless glasses, at a desk just inside the door asked Cletus what he wanted. He said he was looking for a Mary Kalinski, and his hopes rose when he heard her say that the name sounded familiar. She checked an appointment book and after a brief search announced that Mary Kalinski had been in only a few weeks ago to see Ms. Pettifer.

"Could I talk to Mizz Pettifer, please?"

But Ms. Pettifer wasn't in. She had left on vacation with her husband and wouldn't be back for two, maybe even three weeks.

"How long has she been gone?"

The girl said, "She left yesterday."

He swore under his breath, and for a moment or two stood there feeling sorry for himself.

A small group of girls came out of a room down the hall. One, a few years older, said good-bye to them and went back into the room. The others, five of them, all about sixteen or seventeen, in high spirits, laughing at something one of them had said, passed Cletus and went out the front door.

The girl behind the desk said, "Is there anything else we can do for you?"

She was very polite.

From a room on his left came a woman about thirty years old. Dark short hair, stocky, cigarette in her hand. She didn't bother looking polite. Her hard look at Cletus asked what his business was and shouldn't he maybe be on his way.

The girl behind the desk said, "This man was looking for information about a Mary Kalinski."

The hard-looking woman shrugged her shoulders and said that she'd never heard of anyone of that name. Then to the younger women, "I'm leaving for the city. If anyone asks, I'll be back late tomorrow afternoon."

She turned, looked at Cletus as if surprised to see him still there. She asked roughly, "Was there something else you wanted?"

Mostly because he didn't like being rushed out of a place, he said that he was a social worker who had a lot of teenage girls on his case load. He said, "I thought maybe I should get to know more about your program so I could refer some of my girls here. Maybe all of them."

He answered her hard look with an innocent expression that he hoped would convey the thought that it was within his humble ability to deliver to this Women's Center scores of tender, impressionistic, and eager young females. And he succeeded.

She said to the receptionist, "Let him talk to Kay." After which she walked behind the desk, picked up a small suitcase, and left. The girl called after her, "Have a good trip."

Cletus told his name to the girl and she offered hers in return. Edith. Edith Shugrie.

She led him to the room down the hall. As she did so, Edith volunteered the information that the woman he had talked to briefly was the director, Ms. Amy Grouer.

And the girl she was going to introduce him to was Ms. Kay Lindsay. Mostly her job was to do counseling for teenagers.

And that was how he met Kay Lindsay.

It was much like the time he had been picked up by Pamela Treybold, except that Kay was more attractive. Long blond hair, about twenty-one or twenty-two. Nice shoulders. Looked good in faded white jeans and a blue work shirt.

Pamela Treybold had taken him home and treated him very nicely for a day.

Ms. Lindsay took him home with her and their relationship continued much longer than a day. Over the next four or five weeks she sometimes made him so happy that he forgot all about the trouble he was in and how desperately he needed to find Mary Kalinski. Sometimes, with her, he didn't care if he ever found Mary Kalinski.

Pamela Treybold had taken him home because she had thought he was married.

With Kay Lindsay it was because she had been talking with five young women about liberated sex in today's world, listening in turn to their boastful and detailed accounts of how liberated sex was one of the best things a person could possibly ever discover. Each had described the kinds of places, methods, and conditions that best lead to the achievement of almost intolerable rapture. And in Ms. Lindsay had stirred certain physical desires that had gone unsatisfied for some time.

This might well have been the turning point in his life.

Chapter 16

Kay had been talking with a group of high school students about teenage problems, including sex. They had problems enough, she'd found, but sex was not one of them. Difficulties with their families, yes. And school, work, and relationships with adults in general. She had hoped to build the discussion around these subjects, but once they started talking about sex they would talk of nothing else.

But they were gone now, and she sat in a chair by the window and reached for a pack of cigarettes, ready to relax and have a few thoughts of her own on the subject that the young women had been so eagerly discussing.

Edith Shugrie came in, followed by a man she introduced as Cletus Hayworth. Edith said he was a social worker who had come in to see the center and maybe plan to send young women here for counseling. Amy had suggested Kay talk to him.

He was in his middle twenties, serious looking, tall, long dark curly hair, and a mustache that curled down at the ends. College educated, no doubt. Money, probably. But something soft about him. As if he'd been hurt or was in trouble.

Rather nice, actually.

He looked as if he might turn and flee if she spoke too sharply, but her tone of voice was rougher than she meant it to be. "I don't see how we can help you," she said. "This is a center for women, not men."

He said, "I don't mean for myself. I meant for girls on my case load."

Unless you have at some time been on someone's case load, you can't know how much the word grates on your ears. She frowned.

You could tell he knew he'd said something wrong, and for a moment she thought he was going to apologize and leave.

He said, "Maybe it isn't a good idea."

She said, "Possibly not, though I really can't say because you haven't said what it is you want."

He accepted that, grinned like a shy little boy. He said, "You're right. I'm sorry."

She said, "That's all right. But what was it you wanted?"

He said, "Well, I thought you could talk to them about certain things that teenage girls could talk to you about easier than they could to me." And he waited for her response.

After a few moments passed and he had not said anything more, she looked puzzled and said, "I'm sorry, but I still don't know what kinds of things you are talking about." And she waited, amused. Was he afraid to mention the word sex?

He said, "Well," and took a deep breath as if gathering his courage, "sex, for instance. I think they could talk better with a girl than with a man about things like birth control, what to do if they get pregnant. That kind of thing."

She looked at him as if surprised. "You can't talk with them about things like that?" She said, "I thought you were a social worker."

He said, "I talk with them about it, of course." And again he looked like a shy, hurt boy. "But I'm not good at it."

She shook her head, laughed softly, took a fresh cigarette from the pack, and held it in her hand a moment, looking at it, smiling.

He didn't run over to light it for her. That was to his credit. She searched through the pockets of her jeans for several moments before she found a match, but still he didn't move.

(It was not because he didn't have a match, because she noticed a bit later that he got out a cigarette and had matches for lighting it.)

He stood there as if expecting at any moment to be told to get out.

She said, "All right. But I don't think the girls on your case load should talk to girls about sex." And she waited to see how that hit him.

It didn't hit him at all. He looked blank.

"Girls," she explained, "are what fathers hold on their laps. What little boys tease and throw snowballs at. When a female is old enough for sex, she is a young woman."

She blew a stream of smoke in his general direction. "And women shouldn't go to girls for advice." And just in case he still didn't understand, she added, "They should go to a woman. Like me, perhaps."

He grinned and said, "Oh. I guess you're right."

So that was settled. She asked, "What age girls or young women did you plan to send here?"

He said, "I had in mind the ones about sixteen."

She said, "That might be too late." And he looked uncomfortable.

She studied him silently for a moment, then said, "You don't look like the ordinary social worker. I used to think all social workers were old women who thought young women shouldn't know about sex until they were twenty-one. Or married."

He said not all of us. Again the soft smile crossed his face.

She said, "If they came here, we might even give them a talk on women's liberation. Would that upset you?"

It didn't. He said he was familiar with the program and approved of it.

He did seem less the male chauvinist than the average man. He gave a few opinions on the subject and they were acceptable. Most of his opinions, she assumed, he'd got from his sisters. He had three. One was an instructor at Berkeley and into the women's liberation movement there. He talked about her for a while. She was his favorite sister, apparently.

This was the first male she'd talked to for months that she liked. She wondered if he was married. Only out of curiosity, of course.

"It would have been laughable for me to try to feel superior to women," he admitted, "because all my sisters are better at most things than I am. And all make much more money than I do." That thought seemed to amuse rather than disturb him.

He told her of his oldest sister who was a doctor in Albany. She made the most.

To make him feel a little better, she told him that being a social worker had its rewards and he needn't feel bad.

He said, "Thanks. But you don't make much money at it."

"True. But I suppose your wife works."

He said he wasn't married. "But if I did meet someone I wanted to marry, I expect that she probably would want to work."

She agreed. "Probably."

"If it makes them feel more liberated," he said, "it's what they should do."

"All women are liberated. Even the young women you plan to send here are more liberated than you think."

He said, "God, I hope not! Some of them are already almost out of hand." And they laughed together.

"They'll be all right. Don't worry about them."

He said, "I think I will worry about them, if you don't mind. It's my job. I don't want them to get pregnant."

She smiled and again told him not to worry. "Send them in and I'll talk with them."

He said he would.

Then he asked, as one professional worker to another, how she thought the modern approach to sex affected young women. "Can they handle it? All the freedom, I mean?"

She recalled the stories the young girls had been telling in this room less than half an hour ago. They seemed to be handling it very well. She had not yet recovered from hearing about it. And she found that she was looking at the young male in front of her with feelings that she hadn't had for the last two or three months.

"They have their sex and enjoy it," she said. "That's better than feeling afraid and frustrated, like women in past years used to be."

He nodded. That made sense. He said, "I envy them, I guess. Personally, I find it not easy to take it that casually."

He *was* a child. She asked, gently, "Why?"

He had to think about that for a moment. He finally came up with, "I don't think that just using a woman for sex is right. I agree with you that women shouldn't be just sex objects."

She said softly, "That's up to the woman, really, to decide if she's a sex object. If it's something she wants, too, then she's no more the sex object than he is."

He took a pack of cigarettes from his pocket. Took one for himself, lit it thoughtfully. He didn't offer her one. Just looked thoughtful. "Maybe you're right."

Then he looked at her as if he seemed to be seeing her for the first time. He was looking at her in a way that in the past she would have resented. As if he was noting for the first time that she was attractive. But there was also admiration and respect.

He said, "You are very wise, you know that?" And like a typical male he seemed to find it incongruous that a woman could actually be wise!

She only smiled.

"Could I . . . and I don't mean this in an offensive way
125

. . . could I see you after work? Buy you a drink or something?"

She got another cigarette out. Again he did not come running to light it. She blew out the match and looked at him. "I'm going home after I leave here. If you want a drink, you can come there. There's some beer. I don't know if there's anything else."

After he recovered from the shock, he said that beer was what he usually drank and he'd like to come.

They said good-bye to Edith at the desk. Kay led the way out. He didn't rush to open the door. Either he didn't go out with women often, or he knew how to treat them as equals.

Halfway through the second can of beer she asked him if he'd like to come to bed with her and he said, My God yes!

He was a very passionate lover. She had the feeling that it had been a long time since he'd been in bed with a woman.

And later, because it amused her and because she thought it might amuse him, too, she told how the young women she had been talking to had aroused her with their stories of their sex life. They laughed at that. He said that he had been very lucky to have come along at just the right time. Nothing like that had ever happened to him before.

She found it felt good to be in bed with a man again. Better, this time, probably, than ever before. Different, certainly. She felt somehow more detached, but at the same time more engaged. Neither guilts nor compulsions. Just being. As if she could understand that it was only the present that ever existed, and there was no time ever except now, and desire was all, and the feeling of her encompassing him with her body was so good that no existence or future could ever affect the feel of him and her

126

and them and now and more and more and all was very
beautiful, bursting outward into space and hanging there
a small ecstatic moment, then gliding to a gentle, loving
landing.

It was all right. Everything was all right.

She raised her head because he was trying to move his
arm from under it.

She said, "Don't go yet." Then added, "Unless you
have to."

He said, "I'm not going. But I've got to make a call."

She tried not to care who it was he had to call. A
woman?

"I didn't tell you this, but I've got a five-year-old boy
and he's home with a baby-sitter."

She said, "Really? I thought you told me you weren't
married."

"I'm not. Never was. But I got this boy, and his baby-
sitter has to leave by five-thirty. So I'm going to call her
and tell her to go and I'll be right home."

The telephone was in the kitchen, but he talked in a
loud voice and she couldn't avoid hearing his part of the
conversation.

He said, "Mrs. Gogle?" Then, "Look, I'm at the drugstore about two minutes away. I'm giving a friend a ride
home and he's got to stop here long enough to get a prescription filled. So I'll be home in about ten minutes. I
know you've got to get home and fix dinner for your husband, so please go ahead. And ask Hank to watch television for a few minutes until I get there. All right?"

For a few moments he didn't say anything, then, "No,
I'd rather you didn't, actually. Hank will be all right."
Then, "No, that's kind of you, but I'd really rather you
didn't. If you don't mind. I'm trying to teach the boy to be
self-reliant. Not to be afraid. And this is a good opportunity for him to learn. And I won't be more than ten minutes. Maybe only five, even."

After a few moments, "Good. I know how you feel about leaving him by himself, but this is an emergency."

He said, "Good. . . . Okay . . . . Fine. And I'll call you later if I decide to go out tonight. And thanks again."

He didn't come back to bed right away. He went to the refrigerator and got two cans of beer. He put hers in front of her, unopened. He opened his own. She opened hers.

She had missed him, and admitted it. "C'mon back to bed." She patted the place, still warm, that he'd left some minutes ago. And reached out an arm toward him. "Come back for a few more minutes, anyway."

He said, "In a minute. First I got to make another call."

Again she felt a little uneasy. But she only sipped her beer.

Sitting on the edge of the bed, he explained how he'd come to have the boy, Hank. There had been a love affair half a dozen years ago. The first year in college for both of them. The girl had wanted to place the child for adoption, he hadn't. So she'd given him custody of it. His mother had kept it for him until after he'd graduated from college. In fact, until only recently. Anyway, now his son lived with him.

Then he said, "Excuse me," and made his second call.

"Hank?"

Then, "Hey, this is Cletus. Has she gone?"

Apparently she had.

"Good. Now look. I'm not going to be home in ten minutes after all. I'm at the drugstore and was going to take this fellow home after he got his prescription filled, but they don't have the kind of medicine here he's got to have. I'm going to have to go all the way back to town for it." A pause. "Of course not. If he doesn't get it soon, he might die."

After a moment, "Don't be silly. Would I lie to you?"

Then, "All right, now. Stop that kind of talk. Just listen

128

to what I'm telling you. Fix yourself a peanut butter sandwich and a glass of milk. And watch TV."

He was getting some argument from the other end.

"Well, fix something else, then. You can do it. You're five years old, for God's sake. Six next week. When I was your age, I was preparing three meals a day for my widowed mother.

"Okay, don't believe it."

There was quite a long pause now.

"Well, try it if you want. Though that sounds like a big job."

She lay there and wondered what the boy wanted to do. Bake a cake?

"Well, give it a try. Remember, we can always go out to Burger Heaven when I get home, you know."

Then, "Okay, okay. Or just eat cookies. I don't care what you eat. But listen. Drink your milk, you understand? . . . Fine. . . . And if anybody calls for me, tell them I'll be home soon."

He said, "No, just tell them the truth. That I'm taking a sick friend to get a prescription filled."

He finished with "Good. I'll see you soon."

She welcomed him back to bed and pulled him up next to her. "What did he want to do? Bake a cake?"

"No. Just pancakes. He likes them with syrup and peanut butter."

She laughed at that, happily, longer than the joke deserved. It was a sign she was happy. She knew that. She always laughed easily when she was happy. And she was suddenly aware that it had been a long time since she'd laughed.

"He could do it if he wanted to," he said. "Make pancakes. The kid's a damn genius."

Again she laughed, remembering fragments of the phone conversation. She said, "When you get home, tell him your sick friend sent regards."

He said he would.

She said, "It must be tough having a five-year-old to take care of."

He said it wasn't, really. He sounded very serious. He said that he was very fond of the kid. "Sometimes I'm afraid that I've got so attached to the kid that I wouldn't be able to give him up."

That sounded strange. Why was he worried about giving him up? She would have asked, except that he was wanting to make love again and that took her mind off everything else for a while.

He asked when could he see her again and she said she wasn't sure. Not soon, probably. She was pretty much involved with things and people at the Center.

He said, "I'd like to see you again."

But she made no promises. She opened the door for him. "I'll get in touch with you."

He said, "How about me getting in touch with you?"

"No."

"Why not."

It was all too complicated to explain. She said, "I'll call you."

He didn't want to go. She held the door open for him, but he didn't leave.

She said, "It was fun. It was a beautiful time, and I thank you. But you'd better get home to your boy."

In a tone that made it sound as if he were sharing with her a new and rather important idea that had just occurred to him, he said, "I find that I don't want to go. I want to stay here with you a little longer."

She smiled, but shook her head.

"Then you come with me."

She said, "I've got to go to a meeting."

He said, "I'll go get Hank and we'll come back here for a while. Watch TV or something."

She repeated that she had to go to a meeting, and as he stood there trying to think of something else to suggest, she said good-bye again and slowly closed the door between them.

130

Chapter 17

Mrs. Basil called again to ask Cletus to find out what Jeorge would like for his birthday. Cletus said he'd ask the boy the next time he saw him. The next day he reported back to Mrs. Basil that Jeorge would like a Frisbee.

She asked what a Frisbee was.

He explained that it was a thing made of plastic, round and sort of flat, and you threw it to someone and they threw it back to you.

There was a long moment of silence from her end. Then she came back on and asked, "How about a book?"

But it was summer now, Cletus reminded her, and Jeorge is spending a lot of time outdoors, according to his mother. The neighborhood he lives in, the kids play Frisbee all the time.

She asked what neighborhood that was and Cletus told her once more that he didn't want her to get in touch with Jeorge yet. Let him make the adjustment first, he said, without being torn between his new mother and his old one. Very important psychologically.

A week later, a few days short of Jeorge's birthday, she called to say that she had bought a book for Jeorge and she wanted to deliver it to him. Again there was strong disagreement. He said no, and she said yes. She reminded him that Jeorge had been with her for four years, which was longer than he had been with his own mother.

And she had cried herself to sleep every night since he'd been taken from her.

He said, "Believe me, Mrs. Basil, I know how you feel. But I can't let you visit him now."

"Give me his address and I'll mail it."

"No. I'll mail it for you. But that is all I'll do."

She said that she couldn't trust him, and that he was a liar. And again threatened to go to his supervisor.

He said go ahead. And she did.

Mrs. Bok called him into the office. She had the Kalinski file open in front of her. She said she couldn't understand what all the trouble was about.

"Why won't you let Mrs. Basil get in touch with the child?"

He said, "Because the child now belongs to its mother. And the mother resents that we had the boy all these years, lying to her about how he had been adopted. She doesn't like us or anything about us, including the home where the boy was kept. She doesn't want to see Mrs. Basil, or have the boy see Mrs. Basil. And Mrs. Basil can't get it clear that the boy belongs to his mother and that the mother can say who is or is not to see the boy."

Mrs. Bok was impatient with that. She said, "That makes no sense, Cletus. You're not going to be able to keep her from seeing the child. All she has to do is look in her phone book and she can find where the child lives. In fact, I pointed this out to Mrs. Basil. So I don't doubt that she will get in touch with the child and the mother, whether you want her to or not."

Inwardly he groaned. Outwardly he laughed. He said, "Let her try."

"What do you mean, let her try?"

Cletus said, "The Mary Kalinski listed in the phone book is the boy's grandmother. The mother doesn't live there now. She's moved and is keeping her new address secret, as she has every right to do. In my opinion."

Mrs. Bok checked the record. "The address you gave when you discharged the boy is the address in the phone book."

"True. But she's not there any longer."

"Then where is she?"

Cletus said, "That's her secret. And I promised I wouldn't tell." He added, "I don't think we should press the mother too hard. We're lucky she hasn't gone to the newspapers about how we kept her child all these years at the taxpayer's expense, under the lie that it had been adopted."

He wiped a few drops of perspiration from his forehead. And, "If Mrs. Basil does call the grandmother, she will do what Mary asked her to do. Say that she doesn't know where her daughter is."

It was that day, almost immediately after the discussion with Mrs. Bok, that Cletus went back to the Women's Center to see Ms. Pettifer, the woman who Edith said had talked to Mary Kalinski.

Ms. Pettifer was a little older than the other women. Maybe forty-five. A gentle, low-voiced woman, attractive, congenial. Cletus asked her about her vacation. Hoped she'd enjoyed it. She said she had, and told him a bit about it.

Finally he got around to asking her about Mary Kalinski. Did she remember her? And did she know where she was living now?

She answered yes to both questions. She had the address in her book. Had, in fact, planned to visit her sometime.

A pleasant person, she recalled. Quiet. Had had a hard life, especially when she was very young. Many problems. Mary Kalinski had come to the Center asking about free legal services. She had been separated from her husband a long while but had never got around to getting a divorce.

Cletus said, "Divorce? I hadn't heard she'd even been married."

"Yes," Ms. Pettifer said, "she'd been married, all right. Three times. Divorced her first husband, and married

133

again. Then divorced the second husband and remarried the man she had been married to the first time."

Cletus sat there and let waves of depression wash over him. The crushing weight of despair overwhelmed him and he couldn't move.

"I felt sorry for her," Ms. Pettifer said. "She seemed like such a well-intentioned person. She tried hard I think. But she seemed to get involved with the wrong kind of men."

He was exhausted. For three weeks he had waited for this day. And for nothing.

"She wasn't a young woman any longer. As you know," Ms. Pettifer said. "Fifty years old, probably."

Okay, he should have known.

"I remember her well because she was one of the first older women to come to the Center."

All right. All right. No more please. And from some source came the strength to rise. He thanked her, said he had to go.

Cletus had visited his brothers only twice during the last two years. But he corresponded with them regularly. And Faith kept him well informed of their situation.

Walter Hayworth, M.D., was now thirty-six, had an attractive blond wife, three small children, a good medical practice, and his father's low regard for the poor and unenterprising. He lived in a good neighborhood, but not as good as the one he would like to be living in. Would, in fact, be living in, if his youngest brother were not blocking settlement of his mother's estate. He worked hard, played not at all. He was on the board of four community organizations, including the Organization for Community Action against Poverty.

Paul Hayworth was thirty-four, successful lawyer and property owner. He, too, had inherited from his father a low regard for people without either money or the drive to attain it. His opinions of the poor had been strengthened by experience. He owned two apartment houses in

134

the poverty section of Farmington, and his stories of how his tenants mistreated the buildings would tear at the heart of anyone with even minimal respect for private property. It bothered him greatly that there were two other buildings in the same block that he could grab up before someone else got them if it had not been that his younger brother was keeping him from coming into his rightful inheritance.

He had an attractive blond wife and two children. And one child on the way.

It was Paul who kept in touch with Cletus regarding the estate and the money coming to him whenever he was agreeable to accepting it.

He wrote chatty letters. He told Cletus how everyone was doing.

"And the kids are getting big. Wish you could get over here more often to see them. We miss seeing you."

And, "Faith and Karl were here for dinner last night. His ophthalmology practice is off to a good start, but it will be years before he will really be in a position to marry. Faith seems to accept that. No one wants to start marriage without money enough to carry them over the hard spots. So they'll just have to wait. I know she'll feel better when she has her inheritance, as all of us will."

He concluded, "None of us is pressuring you, old boy. Don't accept the money until you're sure you are well enough to handle it properly."

He enclosed the latest report of the estate, which showed that the value of the stocks and other holdings now totaled $506,427.07. Cletus would get five thousand plus one-fourth of the remainder, which, Paul pointed out, was a grand total of $125,356.76.

Faith had called several times. She wanted to visit him in his new apartment, which of course he could not let her do. He made up some really imaginative excuses.

But she hadn't done what she'd promised to do. She

hadn't told Grandmother Hayworth about meeting the old friend on his way to Peoria to work for the Peoria Pure Food Corporation. She said, "I tried to, but at the last moment I lost my courage."

He had to plead with her to get her to do it. "I'm not asking you to do anything that would hurt anyone. I wouldn't do that. But this is a very important experiment I need to make. And you've got to help me."

So she said once again that she'd try.

"And remember what your reaction was. That's what I need to know."

"All right, for God's sake."

So she did it, and called to tell him so. It hadn't been easy, and she'd felt silly as hell. She said, "Okay, so I fell for your stupid practical joke. Now give me the punch line."

He said, "There's no punch line. I'm being very serious."

"Okay, so you're serious. Now what is it you want me to tell you?"

He said, "Tell me what was your reaction after telling that fabrication to Grandmother?"

She thought a moment. "The only thing I remember was that I was aware I didn't know anyone who was heading for Peoria to take an executive position with the Peoria Pure Food Corporation, or any other corporation."

He said, "Good. Good so far."

She asked, "What does that mean?"

He said, "I think it works."

There was a soft sigh from her end, communicating a feeling of despair.

So he reassured her. "It's all right. I'm not crazy."

"Yes you are, Cletus. But it's all right. I still love you. You're my brother and I'll stick by you. But you're crazy."

"All right, I won't argue." And then, "Now there are some other things I want you to do."

"No."

"You've got to. If you really love me, you will."

This time she combined a long sigh with a few soft swear words. "All right. What do you want me to do now?"

He said, "Tell Grandmother you met this long-haired fellow who rides a motorcycle, who came into the drugstore with his girl friend. The girl was young and beautiful and talked about organic gardening and the occult. They ended up not buying anything."

"I won't do it."

"Please."

"Oh, Christ."

He said, "Just try it. And tell me how you felt afterwards."

She did. And again it was not easy. That's what she told him.

He said, "Of course it wasn't easy. But was it easier than the first time?"

"Not much."

"Not much. But some. A little easier."

She said, "Okay, a little."

"Great!" And he asked, "What was your feeling immediately afterwards?"

"Nothing."

He said, "That can't be true. You had to feel something. What was it?"

Impatiently, "Nothing different from last time. That I don't *know* a long-haired boy who rides a motorcycle or a young girl who's into organic gardening or the occult."

Cletus gave a long and satisfied sigh. He said, "I think it works. I think I've got it."

She seemed really worried. "Cletus. Are you all right?"

He said, "I told you I'm all right." And after a moment,

137

"Do you feel there has been any change in your relationship with Grandmother and Aunt Edna?"

"No."

"That can't be. Try to think of what it is."

"None whatsoever."

He said, "Faith, now listen to me."

This was taking place at night. Cletus was in the living room, a can of beer at his elbow, the book he had been reading lying open on the couch beside him. Hank was asleep. At least, Cletus hoped he was.

"You told me once that you felt Grandmother and Aunt Edna controlled the conversation around the house. Remember that?"

She did.

"Now admit that to a small degree they are less in control than before. I mean, you could, anytime you wanted to, interject something about someone you'd met, and their control would be broken. Isn't that true?"

To some extent, she admitted. "But it is not an easy thing to do. Making up some crazy story about a boy on a motorcycle or a man going to Peoria, Illinois."

He said, "Of course it's not easy. But you are only beginning. Success doesn't come overnight."

Overnight or not overnight, she didn't intend to go along with this silliness any longer. Brother or no brother, there was a limit to what she was willing to do for him.

"Please," he said. "This is vital to my well-being. My mental health is at stake. If this doesn't work, we may none of us ever get our inheritance. Paul may not be able to buy another apartment building for years. Walter may be stuck in his small eight-room house forever."

She didn't laugh. But neither did she swear. So he went ahead and outlined the next step.

"This won't be easy. But the next time you are talking with someone, preferably a stranger who you will likely never see again, tell him that the man in your life is an airplane pilot. That he has his own private airplane and the two of you go anywhere you want to go. And if you

138

can work it in, mention that your father was a coal miner from Pennsylvania. Killed in a mining accident when you were very young."

That was too much. "No."

He said, "Yes. For me. And remember, I want to know your reaction. That is important."

"Damn you, Cletus. I'll be as crazy as you are before this is over."

Softly, he said, "Never. You are not crazy and never will be. You are my favorite sister and you are helping me with my research. Because of you, I may very soon be cured and all of us will have a lot of money."

She couldn't promise that she would do it. She doubted that the right opportunity would arise.

"It will, I know."

"I doubt it."

But she did agree that if the opportunity ever arose she would say those things. And he said that was all he could ask. And thanked her.

Before they hung up he said, "You are absolutely wonderful. If I had half a dozen sisters, I'd want all of them to be just like you."

She swore softly and hung up. But happily, maybe. Laughing, probably.

He was pretty sure Hank was asleep. But before returning to his book, he walked to the bedroom door and said softly, "Good night, Hank."

The boy said, "Good night."

Chapter 18

Hank was sitting up in bed, leaning back against the headboard, relaxed, hands folded in his lap. He waited for Cletus to start the story.

This was something new, Cletus reading him a story after prayers.

Cletus said, "Because you've been a good boy, tonight I'm going to read to you again from this book of stories you brought from the Basils."

Cletus sat in a straight-back chair at the foot of the bed. He said, "You *have* been a good boy, haven't you?"

Hank said, "Yes."

"Not *too* good?"

"No."

"Fine." He held up a large book of stories, an expensive book, beautifully illustrated. "We'll read the third story in the book."

"All right."

"And you're sure Mrs. Basil never read any of these stories to you?"

Hank said he was sure.

"Positive?"

Hank said, "Would I lie to you?" And his eyes radiated pure innocence.

Cletus said, "Well, I suppose not," but looked at him suspiciously. "Sometimes, though, I wonder if you always tell the truth."

Hank knew what was coming. It would end with his

getting chased around the bed again. Like the last two times Cletus had read from this particular book.

"It's called *Lemuel the Wise Lemming*.

Already it sounded familiar. The last one had been called *Anthony the Red Ant Who Didn't Want to Go to War*.

Cletus shifted the angle of the book so the light from the lamp hit the pages better. And began. He said, "Once in the north country of Scandinavia there lived a young lemming named Lemuel."

"What's a lemming?"

Cletus said, "Please don't interrupt. Just listen."

He frowned, the continued. "Like all lemmings, Lemuel looked much like a large meadow mouse. Short tail, small ears, long fluffy brown fur. He was, in fact, a very handsome young lemming and his parents were proud of him."

Cletus paused to light his pipe, then continued.

"In some ways Lemuel was different from his brothers and sisters and playmates. Most lemmings always accept everything they are told by their parents and the older members of the community. Not Lemuel. He liked to try to figure things out for himself. Sometimes he agreed with what the elders said, sometimes he didn't. Sometimes he got into trouble because of this. Like the time his parents told him not to eat a certain kind of seed from a plant that grew near their home." And here he had to stop and light the pipe again. It's not easy to read aloud and keep a pipe going at the same time.

"But," he went on, "Lemuel ate some anyway and had a bad stomachache for a whole day and nearly died. And another time when he was told to play only where the other young lemmings played, he disobeyed and found another place that was even better to play. And more than that, while he was not playing that day in the usual place, a mean enemy of all little lemmings sneaked up and caught all of the children playing there and ate them."

141

"What kind of enemy was that?" Hank asked.

Cletus said, "How would I know. I don't know anything about lemmings." And he lowered the book and scowled. "I'm just reading the story. Okay?"

Hank apologized.

"All right. But don't interrupt." He turned back to the book.

He said, "Now I forgot where I left off."

Hank said, "The enemy ate up all the other little lemmings."

Cletus said, "Thank you." And cleared his throat. Then, "One day the whole tribe of lemmings started on a long trip. Sometimes they would travel all day, then stop and eat everything they could, then rest a while. Then go right on again. They didn't stop long anywhere. And they didn't change directions. Just kept going in a straight line."

He shifted the book again to catch the light from the lamp.

"Once," he said, "they stopped at a farm where there was a lot of grain and everybody ate a lot and got fat and strong and full of confidence. They had a big meeting and praised their leaders for leading them to this great land. And their leaders said that there were even greater things ahead and everyone should just follow them. So the next day they took off once more, going fast and in a straight line, not worrying about anything. Just trusting their leaders."

Hank said, "This story reminds me of *Anthony the Red Ant*."

Cletus didn't say anything and just kept on with the story. He said, "One time Lemuel asked one of the elders where they were headed and was told to shut up and follow like a good lemming. But pretty soon they got to where it was sandy and not much food was to be found. But the leaders said they knew what they were doing, and the elders told the young lemmings to shut up and follow."

Hank said, "I thought all of the young lemmings got ate up."

Cletus said, "Not all of them. And don't interrupt."

He said, "If you keep interrupting, I'll not finish the story."

Hank was quiet, so after a moment Cletus continued. He said, "Lemuel wondered if the leaders knew as much as they thought they did. Because he didn't like the idea of simply going in a straight line and faster all the time. He began to lag behind a bit in case he decided to drop out."

He adjusted the lamp behind him once more. "We've got to get a better lamp in here."

Hank didn't say anything.

Cletus turned a page. "Lemuel asked others if they knew where they were going, and was told to be quiet and follow like a good lemming.

"Pretty soon they got to where there were no longer any trees or shrubs or grass, and all you could see was sand. And up ahead, water."

A moment to light the pipe, then, "The leaders didn't even slow down. They ran even faster and yelled for everybody to follow. And everyone did. Except Lemuel. He fell farther and farther behind. He saw the others up ahead go plunging into the water, and not come out again. So he stopped."

He turned another page. "Others yelled at him. Follow the leaders, they said to him. They know what they're doing. You don't.

"But Lemuel only stood there and watched them all go by. And after a while turned and headed back. He told himself that what they were doing didn't make sense. And he didn't see why he should do something that didn't make sense."

Cletus said, "Soon he got back to the countryside, where things were better. He was thin and tired, but the food was plentiful and he ate all he wanted and got a lot

143

of rest. Soon he was fat and strong again, and happy. Almost. He wasn't quite happy because he was lonely."

He turned another page. "Then one spring morning a nice thing happened. Lemuel, nibbling on a grain of corn, looked up and saw a lemming his own age. A girl lemming. She had nice sharp ears and beautiful eyes. Long fluffy brown fur. And nice legs. Her name was Laura. He asked her why she hadn't run into the water like everyone else and she just smiled and twitched her cute nose and said that that would have been a silly thing to do."

He said, "Lemuel knew right away that this was the lemming he loved, and soon they got married, raised two lemmings named Lukas and Lillian, and lived happily ever after."

He lowered the book and looked at Hank. He asked, "How did you like that story?"

Hank said it had been a good story. And he waited a minute, preparing himself.

He straightened up, pushed the covers down a little ways. Then asked, "But are you really sure that story is really in the book?"

Cletus said, "Of course it is. Would I lie to you?"

This was it. Hank threw the covers off and shouted, "Yes!"

And Cletus said, "Why, you . . ." And the chase was on. Just like last time. Around the bed and even under it. Until he was caught and made to apologize.

Chapter 19

He waited for Kay Lindsay's phone call and it never came. He finally called her at the Center and left messages, but she didn't call back. Once he got her on the phone but couldn't get her to agree on a time when he could see her again. Yes, she had plans for the evening. No, not every evening for the rest of her life, and she'd get in touch with him soon.

She said, "I'm very busy, really. I'm very involved with the Center, in more ways than one. It's practically my whole life at the moment."

He reminded her how pleasant their last meeting had been, and she said she remembered. And she'd call soon.

He said, "I love you."

She said, "I've someone coming in to see me in two minutes. I must go."

He said, "I love you."

"I'll call you."

"You won't. I know that."

She said, "I'm very involved with things and people here. And someone is coming in now to see me. I must hang up." And she did.

And that was how it was for a week and a half. It seemed more like a year and a half.

He read in the newspaper that there was to be a panel discussion on abortion at the United Christian Church, and that panelists would include representatives of the legal profession, clergy, civic groups, and women's organizations. He attended that, thinking she'd be there, hoping to get to talk to her. With no success.

She was there, though, near the front, sitting with women from the Center, including Amy Grouer.

He took a seat on the side, near the door, and watched her.

He wasn't the only male in the audience, but he probably was the only male who had come there to try to pick up a woman.

The evening was not a total failure. Not because of anything the panelists said, but because of a conversation he overheard between two women seated in front of him. They were members of a women's liberation group. They discussed a meeting coming up, and one asked if Amy Grouer would be there. The other said she wouldn't. The meeting was Thursday night. Amy was always in the city Thursday nights. Always left here Thursday afternoon and got back Friday.

He remembered that it had been a week ago last Thursday that he'd been to the Center and Kay had taken him home. Amy had been leaving just as he got there.

He thought about that for a while, and made some plans for Thursday.

The panel discussion was unexciting.

Those opposing abortion spoke first. A Dr. Brighton showed a series of slides on the development of the human embryo. He pointed out how early in the development of the embryo you could see the appearance of the eyes, hands, feet. And so forth. His presentation was very clinical and unsettling. No one seemed especially interested, but he talked for quite a while. Next was a Catholic priest who spoke of the unborn child being a human being from the moment of conception. His dry, matter-of-fact manner made the moment of conception and all the events preceding it totally devoid of any excitement or romantic interest.

The third member of the team, a Mrs. Brooker, who represented the Committee to Preserve Unborn Human Life, warned that legalized abortion would inevitably lead to euthanasia and other forms of legalized murder.

During all this Cletus hoped for some trend of thought to develop that would encourage a twenty-two-year-old woman to be receptive to meeting by chance a male acquaintance who had romantic inclinations toward her. But nothing like that happened.

Then those favoring abortion had their chance, and things got even worse.

A professor from the state college reported on an extensive study from Sweden regarding what happened to women who had been forced to have unwanted children. The results were unhappiness in general and an increased suicide rate in particular. Everyone was glad to see him sit back down. But after him came a speaker who included in her argument dismaying statistics on the unreliability of the pill. A look of concern came upon the face of most young women in the room.

Cletus by now felt only despair. It seemed to him that women near him edged a bit farther away. But this might have been only his imagination.

There was only one thing yet to be mentioned that could make things any worse. And the next speaker in some incredible way managed to work into her arguments for abortion some facts on the rapidly increasing rate of VD.

At that point there was not a woman in the room who would go near a man for a week, let alone throw herself into his arms after a chance encounter on the steps.

He waited now only for the chance to escape.

It came when the meeting was opened up to participation from the audience, and the very large woman just in front of him, in a moment of intense emotion, rose to her full height and breadth and shouted, *Give us women control of our own bodies!*

147

And the women on both sides of her arose and echoed her cry.

He slipped out the side door as quietly as possible.

Thursday afternoon he took April McCartney to the Women's Center. April would have preferred some-where else, like maybe out to that little island in the middle of the lake where they could be alone. Or to some lonely country lane. But he turned down both suggestions.

He said, "I've been promising your mother for months that I'd have a serious talk with you about lots of things. Like flunking biology last year, for instance. And staying out nights."

"What does my flunking biology have to do with your taking me to the Women's Center?"

"It's not just biology," he said. "It's everything. Your pride in being a woman, for instance. Your need to get a good education so you can have a successful career. You're a young woman, now, and there's lots you got to learn."

She said, "If there's anything I need to learn, you teach it to me."

Cletus said, "Now stop that. I'm talking to you like an uncle. It's time you learned about things that a young woman can talk to you about better than I can."

She moved her torso about in ways that she knew showed it off to good advantage. "You're not my uncle," she said. "So quit talking like one."

He was in fact her uncle, on her mother's side. He said, "These are good people. I told them I'd get more young people coming to them for advice on health problems, sex, birth control, that kind of thing."

April was sixteen and had been on the pill for a year. She reminded him of that fact. "If you weren't my social worker, I bet you'd make a pass at me."

"Well, I'm not your social worker. Just a friend of your mother's. But I'm not making any passes at you. Not now

148

or ever. But I want you to come with me. As a favor, if nothing else."

It was the least she could do. The most she could do he wouldn't accept. "But I don't want to hear a lot of shit about women's lib."

He said, "You won't have to, I'm sure."

There was a different girl at the reception desk this time. Cletus introduced himself and asked if Amy Grouer was there. When the girl said Ms. Grouer was in New York, he acted disappointed. Then he explained that he was a social worker and had hoped his young friend, April McCartney, could talk to Ms. Grouer. "Are there any other women around she could talk to?"

Yes, there was an Eva Passier and a Kay Lindsay.

"Could April talk to Mizz Passier?"

The girl thought so, and went to see.

April said, "I still don't know why you brought me here."

"Because I like you, that's why."

"You don't show it."

He said, "This is for your good. Not mine. I'm thinking only of you."

She said, "I bet." And looked up at him. "You're going to stay around and take me home, aren't you?"

He told her he couldn't. "I got some important calls to make. And you don't live too far from here."

"Yeh, only all the way across town."

The receptionist came back with Eva Passier. Behind her trailed Kay. Kay looked as if she were on her way out.

Cletus introduced April to Eva and at the same time engaged Kay in a conversation so she wouldn't leave. He said to Eva, "Good to meet you. And this is April McCartney." And to Kay, "Hi! Good to see you again."

149

To Eva, "April is a young woman I thought might like to talk to you and see your center."

Eva said, "Hello, April. I'm Eva Passier."

Kay said, "I was just on my way out."

Eva said, "Come into my office," and April said, "Okay."

"Me, too," Cletus said. "Can I give you a ride?"

Kay said, "Well," and hesitated. "I had some errands to do."

"That's all right. I got some free time."

"It's down this way," Eva said. And April said, "Yeh. Just a minute."

She had turned from Eva and was watching her social worker and the women. She seemed especially interested in the expression on her social worker's face as he looked at the girl called Kay. And a small suspicion started in her mind.

The girl called Kay said, "Are you sure you have time?"

And April heard her social worker say, "Sure. Lots of it. I got the rest of the afternoon free." And heard him say, as they started toward the door, "Quite a coincidence, running into you like this."

The small suspicion suddenly burst into the full-blown recognition that she, April McCartney, had been had. Used!

She said it out loud. She said, "Coincidence, my sweet ass!" And her angry eyes watched until the two had passed through the front door.

Eva said, "Aren't you coming?" She turned and took a step back toward her young client.

"That son of a bitch!"

Eva said, "Beg pardon?"

So April repeated it for her. "That son of a bitch!"

Inside the car, Cletus took a cigarette for himself and put the pack back into his pocket. Kay said, "Stop somewhere so I can get some cigarettes."

He said, "Okay," and shifted gears. Then, as an afterthought, said, "If you're out, I have some." And tossed the pack to her.

Eva closed the door to her office. She said, "I'm not quite sure I know what you meant out there about being used."

April said, "Used. That's what I said. I was used."

That was an odd way of phrasing it, Eva thought. She asked, "You mean by a man?"

April said, "Right. By that son of a bitch who brought me here."

The girl did seem a bit excited. Eva suspected the worst. "Was this maybe something you didn't want to do?"

April laughed bitterly. "You bet your sweet ass."

Eva winced at the crude language, but kept on. "Did you come here because you're concerned that you might have a disease, or be pregnant?"

April thought for a moment. Who knows? She said, "Maybe both."

Eva nodded. This was serious. She said, "I must say that he didn't look quite that type."

And a beautiful thought came into April's head. She said, "I'd be willing to see him thrown in jail, far as I care."

Eva simply said, "Tell me about it."

He said, "I missed you."

She said nothing. They drove in silence for a few moments. "I tried to see you. I even went to a meeting one night, hoping to run into you."

She said, "I know. Amy Grouer said she saw you leaving." And another few moments passed in silence.

She said, "You shouldn't have called me at the office. I told you not to."

That was true. But she hadn't called him, as she'd promised to do.

151

He said, "I love you."

April said, "Where? Just about everywhere, I guess. Lots of times when he'd pick me up after school because he said he wanted to talk to me, we'd go out by the lake where no one was around. Or sometimes we'd just go out to a country road."

Eva asked, "How many times did that happen?"

"Plenty," April said. "Lots of times." Then, after a moment. "He can be sent to jail for all I care. The bastard."

The foul language was almost more than Eva could take, but she was patient. "First let's find out if you're pregnant. Then we'll decide what to do."

April said, "I'm probably pregnant, all right."

He said, "It's been two weeks. Why don't we let the errands go. And just go straight to your place."

Kay was sitting close to him now. Her head on his shoulder. His arm was around her and it felt good. They had pulled over to the curb a few minutes ago to talk things over.

He said, "Let's don't even stop for cigarettes. You can smoke mine."

She said, "All right."

It was all right. It was more than all right. It was beautiful. And she was aware that something new was happening to her and that it was good.

Kay remembered something an older man had said to her not long ago. He said it had seemed to him that he'd progressed through life in stages. Plateaus. And the most exciting moments he had known were when he'd recognized that he had lifted himself up to a new level of awareness. Which was exactly the way she felt at this moment.

She felt different about many things. About herself and other people.

One of the things she'd learned from that older man

was that she had let her past have too much influence on the present. She had taken too seriously the fact that she had come from a poor family and that she'd done at lot of things when she was younger that she shouldn't have done. And that some things had happened to her that shouldn't have happened.

A year ago she would have had to tell Cletus all about how she'd been hurt and what she'd had and lost. She didn't have to do that any longer.

Amy had helped a lot. She wasn't forgetting what Amy had added to her life. And everyone else at the Center who had made her realize that it is not only all right to be a woman, but that it's great to be a woman.

She didn't tell Cletus that she had never finished high school. She told him that she hadn't gone to college. Which wasn't a lie. She did say that sometimes she wished she had gone to college. And was starting to think that she might like to someday. Which wasn't a lie. But she also said that she had come from the usual kind of middle-class family with the usual middle-class moral standards, and that she'd been a virgin until she was almost nineteen years old. And that both her parents were dead. He said his were too.

It seemed all right to say those things because she realized now that there were many things that were much more important than whether or not you were a virgin at the age of nineteen or finished high school. Or once was poor.

And now she had a good man who liked her.
That was nice.

Chapter 20

Mrs. Bok, like most people, had a number of small fears that she couldn't quite shake off. One was that she tended to suspect that things always were worse than she was aware of. Surface appearances were not to be trusted. Though things might outwardly seem to be going well, almost always someone was keeping hidden some disastrous fact that could at any moment break into the open.

Another was that when her downfall did come, it would be because of the long-haired young hippies who were opposed to everything she believed in.

And in Cletus Hayworth was the personification of both these private anxieties combined.

She sighed, motioned him toward the chair next to her desk, and looked him in the eyes.

She said, "Cletus, Mrs. Basil has telephoned me almost every day for the last two weeks regarding the Kalinski boy. And has been in to see me twice."

"Really?"

"That's right." She took a moment to clear her throat of a nonexistent obstruction. "And I assure you that I am not overreacting to what is more than likely simply a foster mother's separation anxiety. I know how much she loved the child and how bad she must feel because he was taken from her."

Cletus said, with a touch of admiration in his voice, "I think you've got it. It's because she can't accept the fact that the boy is back with his mother permanently. That he won't be coming back. That's hard to accept." After a moment's thought he added, "Maybe what we should do is place another child in her home. She could fasten on to that child, and wouldn't miss Jeorge so much."

Mrs. Bok said, "That's a good idea. A *very* good idea."

She made a mental note to put that suggestion into effect at the earliest possible opportunity.

"First, though, let's deal with the problem at hand."

She leaned forward and, in a tone that she hoped would convey how serious she felt the situation to be, said, "Cletus, I have this nagging suspicion that there is something about this case that I should know that you have not told me. I suspect that there is some serious problem of some kind that you are concealing."

The look in her eyes said, Tell me the truth. I can take it.

He said, "The only thing I've kept from you is that the mother keeps threatening to sue us, especially you. Because of what we made her suffer."

She dismissed that as being silly. "That I don't believe." She said, "It is something else. Something that could spell disaster for us if it were discovered." She looked grim. "I *know* something is very wrong about this case and I must insist you tell me what it is."

He shrugged his shoulders. "What is there to tell?" He said, "I can't just make something up."

She knew he was lying. But she kept her voice low and calm. She said, "Incidentally, Mrs. Basil called Mary Kalinski on the phone the other day. She got the number out of the phone book. It turned out, as you said, that the person listed is the child's grandmother. Who, she claimed, did not know where her daughter, the child's mother, is. And maintained that she had not seen her for nearly two years."

She asked Cletus, "Why would she say that, I wonder."

Cletus was laughing. She waited for him to stop laughing, then repeated the question.

"That," Cletus said, "was what she told me she was

going to tell people if they started pestering her daughter. But I didn't think she'd actually do it."

Mrs. Bok looked at the young man in front of her. So typical of young people today. Their long hair, irreverence, disrespect, disregard for common decency. They would destroy the country before they were through. They would someday overrun the world, wave after wave of them, bold and undisciplined, sweeping aside all commonsense rules and customs. You could never trust them to do a thing they were told, never be able to believe a thing they said.

In the back of her mind intruded the thought of retirement. But she fought against it and concentrated on the subject at hand.

"Cletus," she said, "answer me this question. Honestly." Her eyes fastened onto his. "Tell me truthfully, have you seen the child since you returned him to his mother?"

His eyes did not waver. He said, "I will tell you the truth." And she knew that she could believe him. He said, looking her straight in the eye, "Mrs. Bok. I have seen the boy very frequently. A lot, actually."

"Recently?" And her eyes did not loose their hold.

He nodded. "Is yesterday recent enough? I saw him yesterday."

She was disappointed. He was lying after all. "Yesterday?"

He nodded.

"Yesterday, Cletus, was Sunday."

He nodded again.

In a low voice, gently, she reminded him, "You don't work on Sunday, Cletus."

He smiled. "I know."

She asked, "Then why did you see him on Sunday?"

Even before he answered, she knew the answer. And her heart sank. She had been right. Disaster lay just below the surface. She heard him say, "I've got very fond of the boy. And the Kalinskis." And what sounded like

156

an honest admission. "I guess I spend quite a bit of time with the boy."

The mother would be twenty-one or twenty-two. She remembered that.

"Wasn't that a bit beyond the call of duty? Seeing him on Sunday?"

He smiled again, and said, "I didn't do it out of a sense of duty, Mrs. Bok." And they looked at each other without speaking for several long moments.

One of the things a supervisor worries about is that one of her workers will become infatuated with one of his or her clients and have an affair. And now it had happened. As she should have known it would. And she vowed never again to assign a young bachelor to a case involving a young mother.

"Was that discreet, Cletus? Considering that your relationship with the family was a professional one?"

He looked down at his hands folded on the desk in front of him, and smiled. A smile that implied remembered pleasures, satisfactions, happy anticipations. He said, "I forgot about discretion."

She could see how it could easily happen. The mother had been grateful. He had taken advantage of it.

She could picture what his visits were like. The child playing in the backyard. He and she in the house, stripping their clothes off, climbing into bed.

Perhaps when the boy was having his nap. They, in the next room taking their clothes off, making as little noise as possible, fitting their bodies together on top of the covers.

Or probably he even went there at night, when the boy was sound asleep, and they could run around the house naked, or whatever they wanted to do.

As she looked at him now, it occurred to her that he might, in fact, have come to work this morning direct from the bed of the mother, the smell of sweat and sex still upon him.

She suddenly became very angry.

"I won't stand for this, Cletus." She hit the desk top hard with the palm of her hand. "I simply cannot approve of this."

He looked up suddenly and she could tell that he, too, was angry. He said, "Well, that's too bad. For I don't care whether you approve or not." His voice got louder. "What I do on my time off is my own business." He said, "I don't question how you spend your Sundays and I don't expect you to question how I spend mine."

She said, "Please keep your voice down."

And for a while nothing was said by either of them. He studied his hands in front of him, she hers.

Then, "Is this one of the reasons you have not wanted Mrs. Basil to visit?"

He gave that some thought before replying. "Not really. She just doesn't want Mrs. Basil coming around."

Mrs. Bok was now back to using her low, calm voice. "Mrs. Basil said that unless she is allowed to see the boy within one week, Cletus, she is going to write to the governor and ask for an explanation."

She let that sink in. "She is serious, Cletus. She is even asking for a police investigation. And I'm not absolutely sure that I would oppose the suggestion myself."

He nodded to acknowledge that the situation was serious. "I would hate to see that happen," he said. "The whole story would have to come out."

She'd forgot that. Now she, too, looked serious.

"If you are so friendly with the family, Cletus, I should think you would be able to arrange for at least a very brief visit."

He nodded. That made sense. "I'll arrange it. I'll see that she gets to see the kid. You can tell her that. But give me a little time to work it out."

That was good. She liked that plan. They exchanged small, grim smiles and he left.

After he'd gone she turned her swivel chair around and reached into the bookshelf behind her. She took out the policy manual and, just out of curiosity, checked the section on retirement.

You could retire with reduced benefits at fifty-five. Which was what she had thought.

She felt a little better.

Faith called him at home that evening.

She sounded good. Happy. He said, "I'm glad you called. I was going to call you later this evening. How are you doing?"

She said, "Beautiful, Cletus. Everything is working out just beautifully."

That made him feel good. Elated, really. He had known all along that it would work. Fabrication would some day rank along with free association as one of the major techniques in the field of mental therapy.

"I appreciate your doing this for me. I know it wasn't easy for you. I wouldn't have asked you to do it, if it hadn't been so important to me."

There was a long pause while he waited for her to say something. The kind of long pause that implied maybe she wasn't sure she knew what he was talking about.

He said, "Tell me about it. What you said, and how you felt afterwards."

A shorter silence this time, before she said, "Tell who about what?"

"What you said you'd do. Tell some stranger about your boyfriend being an airplane pilot."

She said, "Oh, that." And her tone became apologetic. "I'm sorry, Cletus. I'd forgotten all about that."

He was too disappointed to say anything.

"That wasn't why I called."

"Oh."

She could tell by just that one word that she'd hurt his feelings, so she said quickly, "I did do it, though. What you're talking about. But I'd forgotten all about it."

His voice still showed disappointment. "I wish you'd

have called as soon as possible after you'd done it. While it was still fresh in your mind."

She again said she was sorry. "But a lot has happened recently that took my mind off it. But I did what you asked and I'll tell you whatever it is you want to know."

He said, "Just tell me about it. As much as you can remember."

She said, "All right. I was in that little restaurant on Broad Street. You know, the little Italian place. I don't remember the name."

"Go ahead. I know the one."

"I thought you would. Anyway, I was to meet a friend there, but she got word to me that she couldn't meet me, so I ate alone."

She said, "It was crowded, so before I finished, a man whose name I don't remember—and it's not important— asked if he could share the table with me. And I said all right. And for some reason he began telling me all about himself. And asked me things about myself."

She asked, after a moment, "Are you still there?"

He said, "Yes. I'm listening."

So she continued. "For the hell of it, as a joke, I suppose, I told him what you'd suggested. That my boy-friend was an airplane pilot. I even said that I was planning to take flying lessons myself." And she paused to laugh for a moment. "Incidentally, because he had said he was just passing through town, I told him things I'd not have said if I thought there was any chance I might see him again."

"Like what?"

She said, "When he asked me what I did for a living, I told him I was a model."

Cletus said, "Wonderful. You could be, you know. You're pretty enough."

She said, "He believed me. He asked lots of questions and I answered all of them. Who I posed for, how much I made, and all that."

"Go on."

160

"He asked me if I ever posed in the nude and I said lots of times."

She laughed again. Cletus too. "It was really funny. I wish you could have been there."

He said, "Me, too. But go ahead. I want to hear the whole story."

"All right. I'll tell you what I can remember. There isn't much more."

"Go ahead."

She said, "Well, he talked about how he'd been a salesman all his life and how he thought it was not a bad way to make a living. Though it got lonely when you were on the road a lot. And I told him I was sure it was better than being a coal miner, as my father had been. And about how he had been killed in a mine disaster when I was only six."

"Beautiful!" Cletus said. "My God, that's beautiful." He was very excited. "And what were your immediate reactions after saying those things?"

She said, "Nothing that I remember."

He was impatient with her. "Don't say that. You know better. Now try to remember."

She said, "Look, Cletus, we've been through this before. There are no feelings."

He said, "Faith, my dear sister. Please! Don't fight it. Just tell me calmly and honestly, what were your feelings after you told this man those fabrications. Now try to remember."

She said, "They were not different from the other times. Simply, that my boyfriend is not an airplane pilot. That I was not a model. That my father was not a coal miner."

He asked, in a straight, serious tone, "What is your boyfriend's occupation?"

"Former boyfriend."

"Okay, former boyfriend."

"An ophthalmologist."

"Beautiful. And your father was not a coal miner."

161

"Right."

"What was your father?"

She said, "Stop it, Cletus. You know as well as I do."

He didn't stop, only shifted direction a little. He said, "Did you find it easier this time to talk with a stranger about these things. Easier than you have found it before?"

"It's easy once you get started," she said. "And once you get started you find it hard to stop."

She said, "I told him I had a brother who was a priest and a sister who married a Texas oilman."

They laughed together. Then she said, "But let me tell you about something that is more important than this silliness you got me into."

"In a minute. First, let me say some things about the fabrications and why they are important to you."

He said, "For instance, if a person is to know what he is, he has to also know what he is not. And when you said that your boyfriend was an airplane pilot you knew he wasn't an airplane pilot. Right?"

She agreed to that.

"For the first time you were totally aware that your boyfriend was an ophthalmologist. Not an airplane pilot, insurance salesman, or sculptor."

"Former boyfriend."

He continued. "The bit about how you were going to take flying lessons yourself is interesting. I didn't suggest that. That came up out of your subconscious, and is very revealing. You think about it."

She said, "Cletus," but he didn't let her interrupt. He said, "What you got out of fabrication so far is that you can relax better with people. You've learned that what you say is not that important. You're not so concerned about being judged by what other people think. Whether that salesman thinks your father was a coal miner or not is unimportant. It couldn't possibly at this point make any difference to either of you."

"Cletus . . ."

He said, "That's part of the theory. That you learn what is important and what is not. Some things are unimportant because they deal with trivia, like whether your father was a coal miner or not. Other things are important because they deal with values. Basic principles. And by fabricating you force yourself to recognize which is which."

She said, "Cletus, I want to tell you something."

He said, "If my theory is correct, after a while—after you take the next steps—you'll find it impossible to be anything but honest with yourself. To yourself, you will always know a lie from a fabrication. No more simply conforming, role playing, doing anything without knowing why you're doing it. You won't be able to lie to yourself about anything. You will always know why you are doing what you are doing. And that, my wonderful sister, is the ultimate awareness. The essence of mental health."

He concluded with "And how does all that sound to you?"

She said, "Cletus, I don't think I understand all that, or even want to. Let me tell you what has happened to me."

He said, "When my new theory of self-awareness sweeps the nation, you will be remembered as one of the first pioneers."

She said, "Cletus, I'm not going to be a pioneer. Or a guinea pig. All I'm going to be is gone. On my way. That's what I've been trying to tell you, but you won't listen."

He said, "I don't understand."

She said, "I'm leaving, Cletus. Aren't you going to say anything about that?"

"Where are you going?"

"I'm going to Colorado. That's what I called to tell you."

"What's in Colorado?"

"Sam. I told you about him. I finally called him last night on the phone. Just got his number and called him.

163

It was one of the most exciting, happy moments of my life."

He couldn't help but feel good for her. He told her that. He said, "I'm happy for you. But I'm sorry you're leaving. Right now, especially."

She said, "I'm leaving the store. And Cranesville. And going to Colorado. Just what I'll do when I get out there, I don't know."

"You'll see Sam," he said. "Is he married?"

"No." She said, "Already I've got someone to manage the store. And I'm going to Colorado and maybe finish college. Or get married." She added, "Sam suggested both."

After a moment, "Walter thinks I'm doing the right thing. So does Paul. And both of them will make sure Grandmother and Aunt Edna are all right."

There was only silence for a long moment. She asked, "Are you there?"

He said, "Of course I'm here. I'm just stunned."

"Do you think I'm doing the right thing?"

He said, "Of course you're doing the right thing. What I'm stunned about is that fabrication works so fast."

"Fabrication had nothing to do with it."

He said, "In a few short weeks, with only minimal help from me, you broke loose from your rut, got free of a life you didn't like, free of responsibilities that were more imaginary than real. You saw what it was you really wanted and went after it." He said, "I'm stunned."

She said, "Cletus, it wasn't fabrication. That had nothing to do with it. It was the telephone. Remember? That great instrument? Last night I simply picked it up and asked for telephone information. And when I put it down forty minutes later I was so happy that I cried."

He was so happy for her he almost felt like crying himself. He said, "Beautiful instrument, the telephone. And you're beautiful yourself. I'm proud of you. And for a wedding present I'm going to send you a jeweled princess

164

telephone for your bedroom. Or wherever you wish to put it."

They laughed, and she said, "Thanks, Cletus. You're sweet." Then more seriously, "I don't mean to put down your fabrication theory. It was fun. But the major credit goes to Alexander Graham Bell rather than to you and Freud. If you don't mind."

He didn't mind, of course. He said, "I have some news for you, too." And she asked what it was.

"I'm calling Walter tomorrow. Or Paul, I suppose. To say that I'm ready to accept my inheritance now."

A brief pause before she asked, "Are you sure you're ready for it?"

He said, "I'm sure."

"Good! Then I'm happy for you. I really am. And use the money wisely, will you?"

"I will." He said, "First I'm going to San Francisco to look up some old friends. Then maybe to graduate school. Or into business. Maybe buy a mink farm."

She said she wished they could get together before she left, but that she was leaving as soon as she could. Flying. Direct flight to Denver from Kennedy Airport. But she'd keep in touch.

They agreed they should keep in touch. He promised to send her his address. She said she'd send hers.

They were both happy for each other and everything was wonderful.

And that was that.

Chapter 21

Kay remembered that Hank liked peanut butter with his pancakes, so she put a jar of that on the table even before she made the coffee. She was looking through the refrigerator for eggs and things when he came in.

He was a handsome little boy not yet all the way awake. He seemed pleased to see her. They smiled at each other. She said, "Hi!"

"Hi!"

She said, "My name's Kay. What's yours?"

"Hank."

He was examining her closely, comparing her, she supposed, with other girls who had stayed overnight. She waited until his appraisal was completed, and was pleased to note what seemed to be tentative approval.

It was Sunday morning.

She said, "Your father's gone back to sleep."

The boy got into a chair at the kitchen table and looked at her some more.

She said, "I thought I'd make some pancakes, if I can find the stuff to make them with."

He said, "Pancakes are easy to make." And for a moment it looked as if he were going to sit there and watch to see if she really knew how to make them all by herself. But he got down after a moment and showed her where to find the pancake mix. He said, "You got to have an egg." And got one for her. He said, "I'll break it for you." And did and put it into the mixing bowl.

"Thanks."

"You're welcome." And he got the milk and showed her how far up the cup to measure it. By the time they sat down to eat a while later they were pretty good friends.

She asked him, "Do you always make pancakes this good?" And he said he didn't usually make them at all. "Only if someone is here to help make them."

She told him about how she'd heard his father talking to him on the phone one night and he'd said Hank was going to make pancakes. Hank said he'd told his father that, but didn't do it. He'd made peanut butter sandwiches instead.

"So every once in a while someone like me is here to help you make pancakes?" And he said, "Yes." She said that was nice.

"Too bad your father isn't awake to have some."

He didn't mind. He seemed to find her company adequate.

"Do you know how to play go-fish?"

She didn't know what that meant.

"With cards. It's a card game."

She said she didn't know how to play it. And besides, she had to be getting back soon.

He was disappointed. He said, "It's a lot of fun."

She said she was sure it was. And looked at him for a moment. "Do the girls who stay all night usually play go-fish in the morning?" And he nodded.

She said, "All right. Let's play for a while." And together they cleared off the table, then he got the cards and explained the game.

They talked about things while they played. She asked what he usually did Sundays. He said he didn't do much. His father sat around reading the newspaper in the morning, then they'd have a hamburger and go to the park. Feed the ducks, maybe. Sometimes go fishing. There was a pond in the park. You could fish there if you were under twelve years old. He said he was only five, almost six.

"You like your father, don't you?"

He said, "Yeah," in a long drawn-out way that meant he really did. She could tell, too, by the way he looked. She said, "I'm glad for you."

Then she had to go. He asked why and she said the person she lived with would feel bad if she didn't get back. They, too, read the newspaper all morning, then went into the park or someplace in the afternoon.

"Where do you go?"

She named the park. It was not the one he went to.

"Do you ever go fishing in your park?" And she said she didn't.

"Do you want to go with us sometime?"

She thought for a moment, then said yes.

"Do you want to go this afternoon? My father would take you along."

She supposed he would. But she didn't say it. She looked at the kitchen clock instead, and said she had to go. She didn't even finish the hand of cards. Just said rather abruptly that she had to go.

She kissed him good-bye and told him she had enjoyed meeting him.

He said she could go fishing with them next Sunday if she wanted to, and she said maybe she would. She'd like to. She'd see.

Cletus wasn't happy to find that she'd gone before he'd got up. He questioned Hank closely about what she'd said. "You should have woke me up before she left."

Hank found it wasn't as good a Sunday morning as usual. They went to the store together to get the paper, but Cletus didn't say anything funny or make jokes with the people as he usually did. Twice he asked what it was she'd said before she left. Her actual words. About next Sunday.

Hank asked what they were going to do that afternoon and was told he hadn't decided yet. Except that Hank had to spend five minutes cleaning his room. "You didn't do it yesterday, so you have to do it today."

"Is she going to be coming back again?"

Cletus said, "How would I know. I was still asleep when she left. Remember?

"You just clean your room and don't worry about it. But not *too* clean, understand?"

"All right."

"Not as clean as last time. This isn't any damn army inspection, you know."

It so happened that she *was* there the next Sunday morning. And once more there were pancakes that she and Hank fixed together. And this time Cletus was awake and had breakfast with them. And afterwards they went to the store together and bought the Sunday paper and Cletus made jokes with people like always. And later they played go-fish for a while. And to top it off they went to the park in the afternoon and Hank went fishing and caught fish bigger than he'd ever caught before and everyone had a good time.

At one point in the late afternoon, maybe close to five o'clock, Cletus was sitting by the ice cooler trying to make a can of beer look like a can of ginger ale (because no alcoholic beverages are allowed in the park), watching Kay bending over Hank and helping him untangle his line.

Their heads were bent close together over the tangled line. On her face was love, patience, enjoyment. And Cletus felt happy at the sight of her.

He looked at Hank, at the serious look on the boy's face as he concentrated on trying to see just where the knot started, and felt a sudden emptiness in his stomach as he thought of what it would be like to not have the kid around.

He focused on Kay once more and thought what joy it would be to have her with him every Sunday afternoon from now on.

For the minute or so that it took them to get the line untangled, he pondered on how she might react if he told her that he had a child who didn't belong to him. One that he had stolen, in a manner of speaking, from the Department of Welfare.

She would probably not consider that a very admirable thing to have done. On the other hand, she might say "How nice!" And offer to help him raise the child.

He drank his beer and thought about it.

For the record, this was the first time he had let the thought enter his conscious mind that maybe it would be good if he never found the mother. And whether he was being foolish even to try. But his conscience immediately reproached him sharply for daring to have such thoughts, and he told himself that he had to try harder, much harder, to find Mary Kalinski.

Cletus called his brother, Paul, on the telephone that night and said that he was ready to accept the inheritance. "That is, if Walter thinks I'm ready for it."

There was a soft explosion on the other end, then a controlled but emotional voice said, "Of course we think so, Cletus. We've always thought so."

Cletus said, "Thanks. Are there any papers for me to sign?"

Paul said, "Just one. It's only a formality. Just your signature to show that you promise to spend the money wisely."

His voice gradually revealed his excitement at the good news. "This will make Walter happy. He's been wanting to buy a summer house."

Cletus said, "Good. He needs a summer home."

Paul said that Faith, too, would be glad to have her share of the estate. "Going to Colorado," he said. "Wouldn't be surprised if she got married."

"That always takes money," Cletus said. And Paul said, "Right!" and "Right on!"

Cletus pictured him doing a little jig and waving excitedly to his wife to show that he had good news.

"This will be good for you, too." Cletus said. "I'm sure you can use the cash."

"Well," Paul admitted, "there are a few things I can get, I suppose. I've had in mind picking up some property on the west side that should be fixed up into good apartments for the low-income groups who live in that area. Improve the neighborhood quite a bit."

He added, in a gently reproving tone, "I've missed some good purchases in recent years, of course. But that's all past. And let's not dwell on the past."

Cletus said, "Right." And asked, "How much will it come to? My share?"

Paul said he didn't have the exact figures at hand, but that he'd checked it out only a few days ago and, as he recalled, the portion for Cletus was one hundred and forty-four thousand, two hundred and ninety-eight dollars and some cents.

"That's good," Cletus said. "I could use some cents." And they shared a small laugh across the miles of telephone wire.

"Most of it," Paul said, "is in stocks, of course. Which I suggest you might consider hanging onto. At least until you're more accustomed to dealing with large sums of money."

Cletus said, "I'll do that."

"Good thinking!"

Cletus said, "I'll want some cash, though. I've decided to move to the West Coast within a week or two."

"No problem. How much would you need?"

Cletus thought a moment. "A thousand. To live on until I get established."

Paul said, "No problem at all. I'll put some papers in the mail first thing tomorrow. Sign them and send them right back, and you can have the money in your bank account by the end of the week. I'll send you a certified check for a thousand dollars. Put it into your checking or savings account, as you prefer."

"Thank you very much, Paul."

"You're welcome. And, by the way, what are your plans?"

Cletus said, "Possibly later on to settle in Indiana and get into soybeans. Or to Minnesota and buy a mink farm. I'm not sure yet."

Paul gave his approval of both plans. "And I want to wish you lots of success."

"Thanks."

"And don't forget your family in Cranesville."

Cletus said, "I won't." Then he said, "And I want you to know that I love all of you very much."

"Good," Paul said. "Keep in touch." Cletus said he would, and they hung up.

The next day, Monday, Cletus did two things that were a little out of his usual routine.

One was that he told Mrs. Bok he was quitting his job the end of the week. It was an emergency. He said he had inherited a mink farm in Montana and had learned about it over the weekend. Had to get out there immediately to protect his interests. The present foreman couldn't be trusted. "He'll sell every pelt on the place and pocket the money if I don't get out there and take charge."

She knew he was lying. "You can't leave without a month's notice. Pelts or no pelts, you aren't leaving on a one-week notice."

He said, "The end of the week. I've got to think of my own interests."

She said, "Two weeks is the bare minimum. I can't replace you in one week."

She hit the desk hard with the palm of her hand. Probably swore under her breath, though he would have no way of knowing. Her lips did move a little though. So he credited her with a swear anyway.

She said, "Cletus, I knew the day I saw you that I shouldn't hire you. You're an irresponsible liar. It's not possible for you to be serious about anything."

172

He looked hurt. He said, "That's not true. I didn't used to be serious, but I am now."

Then her face took on a worried expression. She said, "I hope your leaving has nothing to do with the Kalinski case." Her eyes pleaded for reassurance. "It hasn't, has it?" She said, "You aren't in trouble there, are you?"

He said, "Do you mean, is she pregnant?" And said, "No, she's not. At least, far as I know she's not."

He stood up, ready to leave. He said, "Tell Mrs. Basil I'll bring the boy out to see her. So she can see for herself that he's well and happy."

Mrs. Bok said, "I already told her. That's all that's keeping her from going to the governor. And you'd better do it soon."

Cletus said, "I'll do it this week."

She relaxed a bit. She said, "Good. That's good," and went back to the matter at hand. "But two weeks is the least I'll accept."

He said, "One week. That's all. Then I'll be gone. Gone to Montana."

She said, quickly, catching him off-balance, "And taking Mary Kalinski with you."

He looked at her, startled for a moment, then shifted his eyes away. He said, "Of course not."

She sighed, said, "All right. One week." Then said, "But you'd better have all your cases up-to-date before you go."

He promised he would. And started to leave.

She said, "Cletus?"

He turned.

"One thing you should know, for your own good, is that people can always tell when you're lying."

The second thing he did that day that was unusual was to go to Mrs. Kalinski's apartment after she'd got home from work and offer her money. He offered her a hundred dollars.

He said, "I'm leaving town. Maybe by the end of the

173

week. But before I go I need to satisfy my conscience that I tried as hard as I could to accomplish what I came here to do." He said, "I'm offering one hundred dollars to anyone giving me the clue that leads to my finding your daughter."

Mrs. Kalinski had worked hard all day and was tired. They were sitting at her kitchen table and sharing her last bottle of beer. She said, "I don't know where Mary is. I can't even be sure she's around town any more."

"Are you trying as hard as you can to find her?"

She said she was. "I told her friends to pass the word around you're looking for her. None of them have seen her for a long time."

"And you gave them my name and address?" She said she had.

She drained the glass, looked at the emptiness of it, and thought of the weary steps between here and the corner store.

Cletus noted the look on her face and said, "I'll stop by the store on my way and have the boy deliver a couple six packs."

She nodded her thanks. That would be nice.

Then he made a suggestion. "Maybe you should give me the names of her friends. Then I could go talk to them."

That idea didn't appeal to her. She'd rather have the hundred dollars. So she shook her head. "I couldn't tell you how to find them. I'll have to try to see them again myself and tell them to look harder."

He said, "All right. But remember, if anyone else phones or comes around asking about Mary, tell them you simply don't know where she is. And if anyone asks if I had been here, you never heard my name before in your life. Is that clear?"

She was very tired. It had been a hard, hot day at work and she had thought four-thirty would never come. And now this. Some kind of cloak-and-dagger deal that she didn't understand. So she just looked at him with little expression on her face except weariness.

Cletus said, "If you do tell anyone other than Mary's friends, then the whole deal is off."

She was too tired to either nod or shake her head. She just looked at him blankly.

"But if everything works out all right," he said, "there'll be an additional award of still another hundred dollars."

She looked as if she might cry unless he went away. He pushed back his chair and stood up. "But, I have to have the information before Friday. Or I'll call the deal off."

Her shoulders slumped a bit more and her head bent even lower. But she managed to nod, that she understood. And the door closed behind him and he was gone.

At the corner store he got two six packs from the refrigerator and set them on the counter in front of the fat little man in the white apron. Cletus said he'd like to pay for them and have them delivered to apartment 3—B, at number 248. He put a five-dollar bill on the counter.

The man looked down at the five-dollar bill and then at the beer. His expression showed a minimum of respect for either. He said, "We got no one to deliver." And looked up at Cletus.

"I thought maybe you had a delivery boy or something."

The man said, "Not for two cartons of beer." And wiped his hands on his red splotched apron. Another customer came into the store and the man nodded in his direction.

"Take up a bottle of wine with it," Cletus said. And looked at the man. Nothing. He said, "Two bottles?"

The man shrugged his shoulders, motioned with his head toward the shelves where the wine was, and walked toward the back room to get a delivery boy.

Cletus took two bottles of good red wine from the

175

shelves. He picked up his five and put a ten-dollar bill down in its place.

There was arguing coming from the back room. And that bothered him. He hated to be the cause of any kind of trouble. However, this was important. He had to find Mary Kalinski and get her child back to her.

He stood there, looking down at the beer and wine, and was suddenly struck with the reality of what he was doing.

How did he know what kind of person Mary Kalinski now was. Bitter, maybe? Hateful? She was unemployed, apparently. She could even be a prostitute. And on drugs. Probably married to an alcoholic who hadn't worked a day in his life.

Married! That thought jolted him. What kind of father would Hank have? Probably one who put him down, yelled at him, beat him. And the place they lived in would be a horror. Cockroaches, filth, continual arguing and fighting. And in the midst of all this would be the greatest little human being he had ever known. Probably crying himself to sleep every night. And hating his former friend, Cletus, who had kept him from being adopted by a good family, only to dump him back into all this squalor and misery.

Hank. At this very moment waiting eagerly for his father's return home. Hank, who in the last two months had made Cletus into a happy person for the first time in his life. And to Cletus's mind came the scene at the lake, with Hank's head next to Kay's. A happy, loving, secure child. Once lost for seven long days in the woods. And found. And now about to be turned over by his rescuer to people who could never love him. People he could never love.

And this, for God's sake!, had been what Cletus had been about to do. He had been about to take that bright, happy, loving kid up to those two ignorant and miserable people, and say: This is your father and mother, Hank.

Love them!

The door from the back room was kicked open and a boy about sixteen came scowling up to where Cletus stood. The fat little man swept along behind him and up to the counter. He sucked up the ten-dollar bill into the palm of his hand, made some rapid calculations in his head, and said, "Eight forty-eight out of ten."

The scowling boy kicked the counter irritably.

Cletus said, "I changed my mind."

The man's hand paused dramatically, halfway to the cash register. And his eyes slowly turned to where Cletus stood. His mouth moved in a silent prayer for patience.

"I don't mean that I don't want the beer and wine," Cletus said. "I mean that I will take it up myself. Like you suggested."

For some reason the boy kicked the counter again. And the little man slowly finished his movement toward the ancient machine, anger making his face redden. As he handed Cletus the change a coin slipped from his hand and rolled behind the counter.

Cletus didn't wait for him to pick it up. He took the money that had been dumped into his palm and hurried out.

Mrs. Kalinski finally found the strength to get up from the table, get two potatoes from the pantry and peel them. She had just put them on to boil when she heard the knock. When she saw who it was, she moved immediately back behind the table and sat down. She suspected she could best take sitting down whatever it was that was coming next.

He took the beer and wine from the bag, but remained standing.

She looked at the beer and remembered how thirsty she was. She reached out to break a can loose from the plastic piece that held the pack together. She heard him say "I changed my mind." And she turned loose the can of beer and reached for a bottle of wine instead. She didn't look up at him. She was too tired to look up.

177

He said, "I'm calling off the hundred dollar reward." And her hand twisted the metal top off the wine bottle. She looked toward the cupboard where the glasses were.

He said, "Sit still." And took the few steps to where the glasses stood on the open shelf. A moment later he put one in front of her. He took the bottle from her hand and filled the glass.

She saw him take out his billfold. He seemed to be counting the money, figuring in his head. He said something about how he would have plenty by the end of the week. Then he took what seemed all of the bills except one, and dropped them in front of her. There was maybe a little over fifty dollars, at first glance.

She emptied half the glass of wine.

"Forget I was ever here," he said. And she drained the other half.

If she hadn't been too exhausted, she would have laughed. Maybe later. And with an effort that used up most of her remaining strength, she got out of the chair, got him a glass from the shelf, filled it with wine, and handed it to him. And sat back down.

He remained standing, but he reached down and they bounced their glasses gently one off the other. And they drank.

He emptied the glass, wiped his lips, and stood there looking at her. For a moment it looked as if he were going to bend down and kiss her. But he didn't. Just smiled nice. And touched his hand to her shoulder.

"Thanks, Mrs. Kalinski." He set the glass down and left. She refilled her glass once more and sat there enjoying the warm feeling beginning to flow through her.

It was good wine. She checked the label. More expensive than the kind she usually bought.

She counted the money. Fifty-two dollars.

He had seemed like a nice boy. She hoped he'd be happy.

On the way home Cletus had to hear a brief but stern lecture from his conscience. Hank was not his son. He was the son of Mary Kalinski. Should he ever by chance find Mary Kalinski, he must, of course, return the child to her. And he promised himself he would do so. It would be the only honorable thing to do.

Chapter 22

Mary Kalinski was five years old when she heard her mother say that her father wouldn't be coming back any more. So forget him.

Eight years later, when she was thirteen, she ran away from a foster home and made her way back to her mother. There was this man there. Her mother said, "Remember your father, Mary?"

And two years later, when she'd run away from reform school, she again went back to her mother's. Her mother said, "Your father?" And shook her head. "We tried it a second time. It didn't work. Forget him."

Forget this one. Forget that one. Most of the men in her life she'd like to forget.

She was ten years old the time her stepfather, a thin-faced and mean man, had come into her bed one night, naked, smelling of cigarettes and whiskey, and pinned her arms and legs so she couldn't move and lay on top of her and put his thing into her. She had been more angry than afraid, and had fought him. She bit the dirty, smelly hand he put across her mouth. She kept fighting, even after he'd finished what he was doing, and kept screaming at him for a long time. Even after he began hitting her with his fists.

Some days later she learned from the social worker who had come to the house that what had happened had been very bad. So bad that she was to be taken from her home and sent to another house to live. Her older sister and brother didn't have to be sent away, but she did. All because of what had happened to her. Which had been a bad thing.

She was in three foster homes in three years. Always being moved because she kept running away. In the last of the three the younger brother of the foster mother, a fifteen-year-old retarded boy, clumsy, fat, frightening sometimes, had thrown her down in the barn and ripped her clothes off and drooled saliva on her body as he tried to figure out what was what and why it was all so exciting. She told her foster mother, who didn't believe her. The foster mother said that she'd torn her clothes herself and made up the story to avoid getting punished. So she ran away again.

After that was reform school for a year. Then back to her mother.

When she was sixteen, she worked as a waitress that summer at Parkwood Inn in Hartsdale. She fell in love with a boy from New York City who was going off that fall to a college somewhere near Boston. He was very intelligent. He wore glasses with dark frames, was tall and thin, talked about books and people she had never heard of before. He was not very athletic, and sometimes scared of things she wasn't scared of. Like he had never had sex with a girl. She helped him not to be afraid of it. Even to enjoy it. (Not that it had ever before been very enjoyable for her, but it could be enjoyable, she found, teaching it to someone even more afraid of it than you are.)

The summer ended and he was gone a week before she found she was pregnant.

After the baby was born she left it with a neighbor and went to Boston to try to find the father. She hadn't much money, and the third day there she tried to take some food from a store without paying for it, and was arrested. She was sent back to Farmington, found that welfare had taken her baby and said she'd abandoned it. She talked back to the judge when she was in court and got a thirty-day sentence in the Girls' Reformatory in Baldwin. Plus

181

a six months suspended sentence on some charge that she didn't exactly understand.

When she got out, the woman who was caring for her baby wouldn't let her see it, so she waited until the woman was out in the backyard hanging clothes on the line, and went inside and stole her baby away.

She was caught, and this time she was sent away for six months, but first managed to wrestle a policewoman to the floor and to trip up a cop. And punched the judge and broke his glasses.

While she was there she was told that welfare had had her baby adopted. She cried for a long time. A very long time. Later she wrote the worker, a Miss Bliss, a long letter telling her that Jeorge would always be her child and God pity the poor dumb people who thought that just because they gave it their name that it was theirs. She thanked Miss Bliss in a sarcastic way for being such a nice person as to take her baby from her when she was helpless to defend herself.

The year she was eighteen she worked at the checkout counter at the Big B supermarket and shared an apartment with a girl named Darlene Carmel. They had dropped out of high school together, they said, which was a small joke but about the only joke they had during the year they were together. When Darlene got pregnant, she and Joe got married and they found an apartment in the neighborhood. Joe's half brother, Carl Barnes, who used to hang around the apartment a lot, continued to do so after Joe and Darlene left, and after a while sort of moved in. It wasn't the most exciting arrangement possible, but it was better than living alone. And she felt relaxed around Carl. He, too, had dropped out of high school and had spent time in jail. Three months for stealing a car—his second offense—and thirty days for breaking into a liquor store. He hated cops and courts and social workers as much as she did. He was out of work most of the time, but that was the way it was with most of the couples they knew.

Sometimes when he was depressed and got drinking he got mean, and once he came home drunk and wanted money to go back out again and they had a real fight and someone called the cops. But when he wasn't drinking he was all right. He liked to work on cars, his own or his friends', and when his car was running and they had a few dollars to spend, there were good times. They had lots of friends and nobody was any better than anybody else because they were all poor and all of them had been in some kind of trouble.

Once, after they'd had a fight because she said she was tired of him not having a job and doing nothing except work on his car all the time, she packed a bag and left. It was just before her twentieth birthday. She thought she'd spend a few days at her mother's and try to figure out what to do with her life. But when she got there she found her mother drunk and the house a mess. And worse than that—almost unbelievable—her mother was once again living with the man who had once been Mary's stepfather. The one who had raped her at the age of ten and had started all the trouble in her life.

It was more than she could stand. It was so disgusting, so sordid, so dumb. It was so sickening. She left the house in tears and told her mother she not only was never coming back, but that she didn't even consider herself a Kalinski any more. That she'd never use the name, even.

She went back to the apartment and unpacked and told Carl she was moving back in and why. He understood. He said he felt the same way about his own mother. His old lady was living with a man who'd spent twelve years in state prison for killing his brother in a family argument.

Later she heard that her mother had got rid of her one-time stepfather and was living a quiet and good life. But still she didn't go back. And she used a different name.

There was a man at the employment office who always helped her get jobs when she needed them. He was probably fifty-five years old. He was not real tall, was a little overweight and getting bald. But still not bad looking in a certain kind of way. And he was friendly, spoke in a soft voice, and had gentle brown eyes. And a nice smile. He didn't seem to mind when she quit a job he had got for her. He'd always get her another.

She told him she wanted to work under a different name and explained why. He understood, and arranged for her to use a new name except for social security and taxes. The only job he could get for her was waitress at a small diner in the Four Corners shopping center. The food was not good, and she was almost ashamed to serve it. But the old man used to come out there for dinner three or four times a week. He usually came out late when she wasn't too busy. He'd take the booth at the far end and usually she'd have time to slide into the seat across from him and have a cup of coffee and talk with him. Mostly about her problems. Some nights when business was real bad they could sit and talk for a long time.

After a while she got to telling him rather personal things about herself. Once, when she was in a blue mood, she even told about the time she'd been raped. Told him how it had felt and all.

She could tell by the look on his face that it hurt him to hear it. But after a moment, between bites of roast beef, he looked up and asked, "Are you all right now?"

She looked at him, puzzled, and said, "Of course I'm all right *now*!" After all, it had been ten years ago. For God's sake!

He seemed pleased at that, and smiled. He said, "If you want to bring my coffee now, I'm ready for it."

She was angry. You don't have someone tell you something like how they'd been raped and then ask them to bring you your coffee.

She got his coffee for him, but she didn't sit back down.

After a while, though, she got back to having coffee with him on nights when business was slow. And once again got back to talking about things that had happened to her. Like about reform school. The fights there, the bad food. The girls who tried to get you to do things with them you didn't want to do.

And she told how once the man she was living with had got drunk and they'd argued and he'd slapped her hard lots of times and had knocked her against the wall, and she'd got a knife and fought him off. Even cut him up some. And he'd had to go to the hospital.

She could see by the way that he winced and the expression on his face that he didn't like hearing about her getting slapped and knocked against the wall. But he asked the question, "Are you all right now?" And when she said yes, of course, his face relaxed and he was happy again.

Once she told him about having a child and about how it had been taken away from her and adopted, and tears came to her eyes. That time he didn't ask if she was all right now, he just held her hand and looked unhappy.

(It was much later, after she quit her job and moved in with him, that she understood what he was trying to say to her.

One night, after they had sat up late talking about a lot of things, and were in bed and he had already fallen asleep and she was just at the point of doing so, she suddenly felt maybe she understood, finally.

She reached over and shook him until he was about half awake. She said to him, "There was one time when I was only thirteen and a retarded fifteen-year-old boy threw me down hard and tore off my clothes. It was in a

185

barn on a farm where I was living." And she waited to hear what he would say.

Maybe he wasn't even half awake. Maybe about a quarter. The words came out so slow and fuzzy. He asked, "Are you all right now?"

And she turned over on her back, smiled, and her whole body relaxed. She said, softly, "Yes, I'm all right now."

He muttered something that might have been "That's good," and was back asleep.

She lay there feeling light as a feather. She could have wafted up to the ceiling if she'd wanted to, and slowly drifted back down.

She said aloud, again, "Yes, I'm all right now."

She felt very happy. Before she let herself fall asleep she bent toward him and touched his cheek with her hand and kissed the back of his neck.)

Finally she found that she'd had all she could stand of seeing her wages and tips spent to buy parts for the old red Plymouth in the backyard that was always broken down. And a man who couldn't or wouldn't hold a job. Bills, arguments, beer cans, and not much else. She told Carl to get a job or leave and he said he didn't plan to do either. So she packed two suitcases, left a note for him to find when he got home from trying to find a used fuel pump, or something, and went to work. Just where she'd go after she got off, she didn't know. But she'd find a place somewhere.

She mentioned this latest problem to the old man that night, and he said she was welcome, if she wished, to use a back bedroom in his house until she found a place. And because she had nothing better, she accepted the offer.

He lived in a small village just south of Hartsdale. About twelve miles from Farmington. About a quarter mile off the main road, in a small wooden frame house among the trees. He lived alone. He had three children. Two daughters in California and a son in the Peace Corps in Liberia.

For four days she worked her regular hours at the diner and he brought her home after she finished. She even looked in the newspapers for rooms or small apartments to rent. On the fifth morning she sat in the backyard and listened to the sounds of the birds and watched the squirrels make quick, confident leaps from one tree branch to another, and she knew she couldn't go back to Farmington and the diner.

She called her boss and told him she wasn't coming in any more.

The old man didn't mind. She could live there, he said. If she wished. There was work enough around the house for her to do, and he would pay her to do it.

A few days later, while he was at work, she moved the bureau from the back room into his bedroom and put her things into it. And hung her clothes in the closet alongside his.

That made him very happy.

Those were good days. It was a pleasure to look out the back window and not see a partly torn down old car in need of some expensive repairs, and it was good to have someone tell you how beautiful you are. What other lovers had hardly bothered to notice, he saw as almost unbelievably perfect. For the first time in her life she knew what it was like to be admired. Loved.

The old man had a lot of books to read and records to listen to. She used to look forward to his coming home, and she'd have a drink ready for him and they'd talk of what she'd read that day or listened to. Most of the books she found hard to read, but he helped her. For the first time she found she wanted to know more about everything. He said, "It's all there," pointing to the bookshelf. "In those books. Though sometimes the authors don't know it." He said many things like that that she didn't understand.

He was different from what she had guessed he was. And did strange things.

He taught her one strange thing.

In the morning, sometimes, he would walk into the yard and say out loud, "Hello, trees!"

The first time she heard it she thought he was a little crazy. Then he had her try it. He said you have to say it out loud and mean it. And if you can do it, and mean it— *really* mean it—you will understand the meaning of life. More than that, the meaning of it all.

She got pretty good at it.

"Hello, trees."

He said it worked also for grass, or bushes, or weeds. Rocks, even. Anything.

If any of her friends from Farmington had seen her, they would have thought for sure she was wiped out. If they'd seen her there, her hand, palm up, just under where the tip of the pine branch bends down. Touching it the way you would a human being, gently. Letting it rest there, and saying out loud, "Hello, pine tree."

It didn't last, of course. Good things never do, it seems.

She gradually met young people her own age. They were different from the kind she'd met before. Sometimes they, too, had broken-down cars in the backyard, but they also had gardens they tended in a particular way, made candles or pottery, worked at whatever they felt was honest labor. The wives did weaving or worked at jobs in town or whatever they wanted to do. And she learned from them things she hadn't known about before, like how important it was what month of the year you were born, and what a tarot card was. And what kinds of food were better for you than other kinds.

The old man liked her making friends with people her own age in the area. He encouraged her. He went with

188

her after dinner to places where there was music and dancing and didn't mind if she danced all evening.

Sometimes when she came back to their table, exhausted, flushed, and laughing, on the arm of someone her own age, she saw in his eyes a look of fear, almost, and she knew why.

She would sit down next to him and with her fingers turn his face to hers, and say, "Don't worry, old man. I love you." And kiss him.

He was killed that spring. In late May, about the time the leaves had formed on the trees and the daffodils in bloom and the birds so thick with song that anything other than coming alive was almost impossible to accept.

She heard about it on the radio an hour after it happened. It was late morning and he was on his way back to his office from an appointment in Glenbrook. A police car chasing a speeding driver swung out too wide on a sharp curve and hit him almost head on.

He died by the side of the road, even before the ambulance got there.

For the first half hour she cried. For the next hour she tried to think what to do. And cried each time she found herself wanting to ask him to tell her what to do.

She knew, of course, what he would have said. He would have said, do what you want. It's all right.

The children would be coming back, of course. The daughters from California. The son from Liberia.

Because somehow it seemed the fitting thing to do, she went through the house and removed the signs of her having been there. She even took some things back to the woods and buried them there. She packed two suitcases with clothes and other things, took some books that she knew he would have wanted her to have. Some small trinkets of a sentimental value. And the money he had given her for groceries. She would need that.

A few times the phone rang, but she didn't answer it.

It was late afternoon by the time she got to the highway. She was picked up almost immediately by a dark-haired, stocky woman about thirty years old, who got impatient with her because she broke into tears during the ride. The woman asked bluntly if it had to do with a man, and, of course, in a way it did, so she nodded.

"Then you're wasting your tears," the woman said. "And stop it right now."

The woman pulled some tissues from a box in the glove compartment and thrust them into Mary's lap. "No man is worth crying over."

Which only made it worse.

The woman introduced herself as Amy Grouer. "And what's your name?"

She gave the name she'd used at the restaurant.

She said, "Kay Lindsay."

Amy said, "Where are you headed for?"

Kay shook her head.

Amy said, "Does that mean that you aren't willing to say, or that you don't have any place to go?"

She nodded.

"You mean you don't have any place to go?"

Kay nodded again.

Silence for a moment. Then, "Do you have any money?"

She said, "Some."

The woman was impatient again. "I know you have some. I assumed you have at least a dime. What I want to know is how much? A hundred dollars? Two hundred?"

Kay said, "About eighteen." Kay used one of the tissues. Straightened up a little more in the seat and tried to get her feelings under better control. "Maybe nineteen or twenty."

"Do you have a job?"

She blew her nose softly, and shook her head.

"Do you plan to go back to the man you are leaving?"

That started her crying again. But she shook her head.

190

Amy said, "One more question, then I'll let you alone." And she asked, "Were you married?"

"No."

Amy took another handful of tissues and dumped them into Kay's lap. She ordered her to dry her silly tears. Everything had probably been for the best. And not to worry.

After a while Amy outlined the way things were to be. She said that she had an extra bedroom. "You can sleep there until you pull yourself together. You can get a job and find your own place in due time, if you wish. Or you can stay."

Amy drove fast. Mary wanted to ask her to slow down but was afraid to.

"There are some things I have," Amy said, "and some things I don't. Patience I don't have. Money I do."

She lit a cigarette while going around a curve. "Inherited from my father a few years ago. Half of Grouer Brothers. Office equipment. Father and my uncle owned it together. I go to the city every Thursday and stay over for a meeting Friday morning. But that's my only involvement with the business."

She concluded with "I'm on my way back from there now."

Nothing more was said until they pulled up in front of the apartment. Amy got out, took both of Kay's bags and said, "C'mon."

She had to decide whether or not to go to the funeral.

She knew what he would have said. Do whatever you wish. Either way is all right. And for the next few days she thought about it. The funeral was delayed until the son could get back from Liberia, so she had an extra day to make up her mind.

She finally decided not to go.

Which was all right.

She stayed with Amy, and it worked out well enough. She felt she couldn't go back to the employment office, ever. Or back to the diner where she'd worked before. Or even back to being a waitress.

Amy was director of the Women's Center. It was her whole life. She had Kay as a volunteer worker for a while, then began paying her a small salary. And there was a lot to learn. To Kay, it seemed almost like the logical next step in her life. After a while she found she liked the job.

It was a relief, too, to be around only women for a change. Sometimes when she thought back on all the pain the male sex had caused her— starting at age ten— she understood why the feeling against men was so strong at the Center. The other women, also, in one way or another, had been hurt by men.

She found Amy different from what she had at first thought. Not nearly as tough or hardened as she appeared to be. Sometimes when they were alone at night Amy cried, even, about the unhappiness she had known. Disappointments, other things that had hurt her.

Kay would hold her in her arms and ask, "Are you all right now?" But it didn't work. She couldn't do it right. She tried to convey how it was that everything was all right, that you have to know disappointment to understand what satisfaction is like. Unhappiness to know what happiness is. Frustration to know fulfillment. And that it was good that things happened to us that we hadn't planned or wanted. That if we had the power to choose our own experiences we would see that only nice things happened. And end up weak and afraid as a result. But she couldn't quite remember the whole formula and after a while gave up trying.

Chapter 23

It had been a long time since Amy Grouer had missed being at Uncle Ben and Aunt Judy's place for Thursday night dinner. Months, probably. She would call them soon and explain that she wouldn't be there tonight. But she didn't want to call them right now and risk being on the phone when Cletus Hayworth walked in. She wanted very much to see the expression on his face.

They were in the kitchen, Amy and Kay, a glass of beer in front of each of them. It was three o'clock in the afternoon. Neither had spoken for several moments. Their conversation during the last half hour had been marked by just such periods of strained silence.

Kay broke it this time with "I keep coming back to what I said before. That you somehow make it appear that I am disloyal, when there had never before been any mention of loyalty. It wasn't one of the things that you asked of me."

That was true. Amy had agreed to that earlier. She felt no need to comment on it again.

Kay said, "You told me rather specifically, if I recall correctly, when you picked me up that day, that you had an extra bedroom. And that I could stay, or go, as I wished. It was simply a generous offer to provide a place for me to stay until I was able to take care of myself again."

Amy said, "True. I said that."

"You simply said that there was an extra bedroom.

You didn't say that there were certain things I might do in it that you'd object to."

That was cruel, and Kay recognized it. She extended her hand a few inches toward Amy and said, "I'm sorry. I didn't mean that quite the way it sounded."

Amy reached out her hand and covered Kay's. "It's all right."

Brief silence, broken again by Kay. "I'm sorry that he calls me at the Center. I know he shouldn't do that. I asked him not to."

Amy said, "I can't object to that. He's a free citizen. If he's got a dime, he can call anyone in town."

But now they were being silly. Whether or not he called her at the Center wasn't important. And again Amy tried to think how to get their disagreement focused on what it was that was really crucial. That caused the sick and empty feeling in her stomach.

Kay said, "I'm free, too. That's what I've been trying to tell you. Free to stay out all night, sometimes, if I want to. I'm twenty-two and free."

That, too, had been discussed.

"It's been a long time," Kay said, "since I had to call home and ask if it was all right if I didn't get home by midnight."

Amy said, "Let's not talk about that any more, all right?" And she got up, got two more cans of beer from the refrigerator. She opened both and set one in front of Kay.

Amy remembered a slogan that had been on the wall of her father's office. Directed at the sales staff. It read: YOU CAN'T WIN THEM ALL. JUST DON'T LOSE ANY.

And that was what was the underlying, unspoken, subject for today. Losing. Something Amy didn't like doing. And wasn't good at.

She had lost her mother at the age of three, along with the new baby brother she had been promised.

194

And the brother she'd already had she lost when she was nine and he was twelve.

She lost the role of high school valedictorian by a fraction of a point. Just as it seemed she always lost a spelling bee by a single letter or the running broad jump by half an inch.

She had dropped out of college to marry a man whom she admired because he never lost. Whether on the playing field, in the executive suite, or in the bedroom. Handsome, hard driving, born winner. And she'd lost him two years later to a woman whose hair was a shade shinier, smile a gleam brighter, legs a touch shapelier. And two years younger.

Once she said she wished she were a masochist so she could enjoy losing. She did it so much.

She'd lost everything except her half share of Grouer Brothers, Inc., that her father had willed to her.

Yes, she had lost him, too. Her father. Three years ago.

And now she might lose Kay. But not without a fight.

Amy said, "The thing you mentioned first, going away for a while. That might not be a bad idea after all."

Not good, but certainly better than what appeared to be the other alternative. Cletus Hayworth.

Kay nodded. "I think you're right. I need to get away. I've been taken care of too long." She said, "I used to be very independent, but I'm not any more."

Amy said, "Then do it! Go. Leave your things here and come back when you're ready."

Kay said, "That's not the way I want to do it. I want to give away everything except what I can carry. And I want to hitch out to the coast. Or some place else. Far from here. And work again. And not rely on anyone." Then she added, "Unless I want to."

There was an implication there somewhere that made Amy tighten up. She said, with sarcasm in her voice, "Like some man, you mean. One who needs a housekeeper." She said, "Maybe that's the kind of freedom you want."

Kay reacted to the sarcasm. She said, "That's not a bad idea. Preferably one with a good income."

Amy got scared. And fear made her angry. It always had. She said, "Then go, dammit!" And hit the table with her fist. "If you don't feel you're free here, then go on."

She remembered that Friday afternoon on the way back from the city that she'd picked up this frightened and weeping young woman with all her possessions in two suitcases. And practically no money.

She said, "Find yourself a man again who'll support you. Maybe it will turn out different than it did the time I picked you up on the road a few months ago."

It's wonderful how anger can make you feel better. You don't feel like a loser when you're angry. "Or move in with your friend, Cletus. If you like."

She waited for Kay to say something, but nothing came.

"If he'd have you," Amy said. And the anger increased.

She had done so much for this woman, and now this was what she was getting in return. She had opened her home to her, and now had found that she used it in her absence as a place to bed down with Cletus.

"He may kick you out, of course, if he finds himself a fifteen-year-old girl to replace April McCartney."

Kay said, "Stop it, Amy. I don't want to talk about it."

Amy said, "Oh, you don't? You think maybe Eva Passier was lying?"

Kay put her hands over her ears and refused to listen. But Amy forced her to. She said, "Fifteen was all the girl was. Fifteen years old."

"Sixteen."

"Sixteen now, maybe. But fifteen when they first started. And he'd still be using her if it weren't that she was afraid she was pregnant."

Kay shouted, "Stop it!" and rose half out of her chair.

Her lips formed a tight thin line and her eyes flashed a warning. Then she sat down again, and after a moment said, "Let's don't talk about it. Please."

Amy relaxed. The anger left as quickly as it had come.

She said, lovingly, "It's just that you are too good a girl, Kay, to get involved with a sexist pig." And she offered Kay a cigarette before continuing. "I'm too fond of you to see you hurt."

Cletus stopped by Mrs. Bok's office to say that he wasn't feeling well and was going to take the rest of the day on sick leave.

She wasn't surprised. She asked, "Are you coming in tomorrow?"

He said, "Tomorrow? Friday? That's my last day. I wouldn't miss that, of course. Unless," he added, "I'm coming down with the flu or something."

This would be the last time she'd see him. She knew that. Tomorrow he'd call and say he wasn't well. "Sorry to miss having lunch with all of you."

"Did you finish bringing all your cases up-to-date?"

He said, "Every case. Everything."

"And the Kalinski case?"

He nodded. "Taken care of. I've promised Mrs. Basil I'll bring the boy out for a visit before I leave the area."

She wondered if he really would.

Then she looked into his eyes and in a tone that expressed not criticism, but friendly concern, said, "Are you sure that taking Mary Kalinski and her child with you is the wise thing to do?"

The directness of her question caught him by surprise. Then a guarded look came over his face as he no doubt tried to decide whether or not to tell the truth. She saw guilt and confession there. Then he said, "How could you suspect a thing like that, Mrs. Bok?"

She said, "I suspected it from the beginning, Cletus. I'm not sure, though, that you are being wise."

He looked thoughtful. Shrugged his shoulders. "Who knows."

She asked, "Is she attractive?"

"Very."

"Aren't you concerned about taking on the responsibility of a six-year-old child?"

She was pleased to see that he at least looked serious. It appeared to be something he had given some thought to. He said, "I'm a responsible person. I didn't used to be. But I am now."

She said, "Do you have enough in common, you and the mother?"

"Enough."

She said, "Really, Cletus! I think you are being very foolish. But I doubt if there is anything I could say that would make you change your mind."

She said, "I suppose you think you are very much in love. And maybe you are. But still I think you are making a mistake."

He said, "I am in love, Mrs. Bok. Very much. That is the truth."

What more could she say? Nothing, really. So she held out her hand. "Good-bye, Cletus. And good luck."

He said thanks, and good-bye to her too. Then he was gone.

So that was that. He had been a good worker. Despite his long hair and hippy ways, she actually felt rather kindly toward him.

She hoped he would be happy.

The only person he stopped to chat with on his way out was Thelma Howlett, a small, slender, intelligent young woman about twenty-four. She had been there only six months, but they had become good friends. She and he had snatched at brief moments to talk of life and the fascinating complexity—but compactness—of it all. She worked very hard, drove herself to meet every challenge, almost as if she needed to prove something. Which, of course, she didn't. She was the one Mrs. Bok would now turn to with the tough assignments.

She had a two-year-old child. And a twenty-seven-year-old college graduate husband to care for it. He didn't like to work. She did. He did the housework, laundry, fixed the meals, cared for the boy, read Zen, and toyed with whatever fad or intellectual diversion was popular with the young, liberated crowd they were part of. She was happy with the arrangement.

He sat at her desk for a moment, said he was going home for the day with a headache. She understood. It was what she, too, would do if this were her next to the last day. "And you're probably not coming in tomorrow, are you?"

He admitted he wasn't. He hated good-byes. And farewell lunches. He said, "I'm coming down with the flu."

She said, "I'll miss you. The place will be less fun without you."

"Thanks. I'll miss seeing you."

That was nice, too. "Thanks."

"I hope everything works out for you." He tried to fight back the picture that came to mind of her here at fifty, sitting at this desk, filling out some papers, glancing at the clock, wondering how to make the rest of the day go a bit faster.

"Did you really inherit a mink farm? Mrs. Bok has been telling us that you said you did."

He admitted that he hadn't told Mrs. Bok the truth. "I'm going to California. San Francisco, where I lived three or four years ago. I still have some friends there. After that, I don't know." He said, "I'll send you my address after I get out there. You and Mike and Mike, Jr., might want to come out for a visit."

The idea was good, but she doubted if they'd be able to do it. And she asked if he was going out by himself. He said he wasn't. And suddenly he wanted to tell her about Hank and everything, but he didn't. He only told her that he had met a girl about a month ago who was going with
199

him. He didn't say that he had not yet asked the young woman if she wanted to go. "The first woman I ever met," he said, "who I really love. And would like to be around for the rest of my life."

She was happy for him. They agreed that being in love was wonderful.

"I love her very much."

She thought that was beautiful. "I'm sure she loves you very much, too. And I'm sure she'll do all kinds of good things for you to make you happy."

Then he said he had to go. He was on his way right now, actually, to see the girl he loved so much. But don't tell Mrs. Bok. And they shared a small laugh. They touched hands, and he left.

He had liked Thelma very much. One of the good ones. He could have loved her, too. And he hoped she would be happy.

He picked up a bottle of wine for his rendezvous with the woman Thelma had predicted would do all kinds of nice things for him. But what she did turned out to be something not very nice at all.

And what her friend Amy Grouer did was not very hospitable.

He knocked, and pushed open the door. And the first thing that caught his eyes was Amy, sitting across from Kay. On Amy's face was a look of amusement and triumph.

She said, "What a surprise! Come on in."

For a moment he could only stand there, unbelieving. The look of happy anticipation on his face drained away. But he finally pulled himself together enough to close the door. Or, rather, to try to. It had jammed on the small rug beneath it. He kicked at the rug, which made it bunch up even more. Then he bent down and straightened it so it would lay flat, and the door closed over it.

It was not a great entrance.

There were empty beer cans on the table, so they had

been here a while. And the ashtray was full of cigarette butts. And from the way they looked at him he felt pretty sure that he had been the main topic of discussion.

He did his best. He tried several things.

He said, "I'm sorry I'm late. But I ran into this girl in the liquor store that I hadn't seen since high school. An actress, now, and making it big in New York."

He got three glasses from the cabinet and set them on the table, but poured wine only for himself. He said, "Help yourself." And took a sip.

Amy declined. But Kay said, "Thanks," and filled a glass.

To Amy, "Looks a bit like you," he said. "But not as attractive. And heavier."

He turned to Kay. "How've you been. Haven't seen you for a while."

She said, "Fine." And added, "Amy intercepted your message saying you'd be here at three."

Amy objected to its being phrased that way. She said, "I didn't intercept your message. I simply happened to see the message Edith left on your desk." She said, "You make it sound as if I went through your mail."

"Not through my mail," Kay said. "Only what's on top of my desk." And they exchanged glances that were less than real friendly.

Amy filled her glass with beer, and settled herself more comfortably in her chair.

One thing was certain. Amy wasn't about to say, "Now that you're here, Cletus, I'll leave so you two young lovers can be alone. And use my bed if you think it's more comfortable."

Amy said to Cletus, "I assumed you were going to have a party. So I joined you."

He said, "Good, Amy. Glad you're here. I been hoping for a chance to rap with you sometime. I got a sister in Berkeley who runs a women's center there. Mentioned you to her in my last letter."

201

Kay said, "Please, Cletus. Let's not get started on your sisters."

The tone of voice hurt. Cletus said, "Okay. Sorry. Didn't realize it bothered you."

"It doesn't bother me," she said. "But it does get tiresome. You do it so much."

After that there was a small period of silence. Cletus had some more wine. Then he put the glass down and said, "The reason I wanted to stop by was to see if you two felt like eating out tonight."

Amy answered. She said, "Kay and I are going to eat in. But if you feel like eating out, don't let us stand in your way."

He turned and asked Kay. "Do you feel like going out to dinner with me?"

She said, "I don't think so, Cletus. I'm not in the mood."

So things were really bad. He had more wine and tried to think of something else.

He would have tried levity, but he couldn't think of anything that could get a laugh under these circumstances. And the same feeling came over him that he'd felt the night at the panel discussion on abortion. Depression.

So he filled his glass again.

Amy said, "One thing your sister should have told you is that women don't need to have men take them out to dinner. Women are perfectly capable of taking themselves out to dinner."

He felt something shift inside, like a dam cracking a little. Threatening to give way. But not quite.

"Men take women out to dinner the way a child plays with a toy. A grown toy. To be fed and said nice things to. Shown off. Bribed with a meal and some drinks." She said, "I'm surprised your sister in Berkeley didn't explain that to you."

He sat there thinking of the things he had wanted to

202

talk with Kay about. And one of those things was that he didn't really have a sister in Berkeley.

He'd planned to tell her that he had only one sister, who was about to leave—or perhaps had already left—for Colorado.

Another thing he had wanted to tell her was that the little boy she liked so much didn't belong to him. And that he needed to get out of the area before people found out. And how the boy needed a mother, and maybe she'd find it fun being that for him.

And he wanted to tell her that he had a lot of money now.

And other things. Like how he was tired of handing her cans of beer unopened. And that he'd like to light her goddam cigarette sometimes.

And that he loved her. He'd planned to say that several times. And would she come to California with him?

Amy said, "Every man thinks that all he has to do is wave a few dollars in a woman's face and she'll be his slave."

The dam didn't burst. It just sort of gently gave way.

Cletus reached out for the wine bottle. He filled Kay's glass, then set the bottle down. He picked up Kay's glass and lifted it up to her.

She didn't take it right away. Just looked at him. Then said, "What's that for?"

He shrugged his shoulders, and smiled. "I don't know. Just something I wanted to do. I'd like to pour your wine and light your cigarettes from now on. And do all kinds of nice things for you."

He would never know whether she would have taken it or not. Because Amy grabbed it and threw the glass across the kitchen. The wine splattered all three of them, and the glass broke against the bottom of the cupboard.

And the silence that followed was even heavier than before. And no one moved.

Cletus broke the quiet. He said, "I don't think I want to stay here. But I want to talk to you, Kay. Will you come with me someplace? I've some serious things to ask you."

She shook her head, not angrily, but just to say that she didn't want to.

"I'd like very much for you to."

She shook her head again. Then she said something real crazy. She said, "If you want to go somewhere, why don't you go tell April that she's not pregnant." She looked at him. "And she's not got VD or anything."

He looked at her and tried to figure out how in hell that had come into the conversation. That April McCartney wasn't pregnant.

But what she had said did have an effect. For the first time he realized that he was really free of the burden of giving a damn whether April or any of the other girls on his case load was or was not pregnant. Or on drugs. Or dropping out of school. It was a great feeling of relief. And he shared it with her. He said, "I don't have to be concerned about April any more. I don't need to worry whether she is or isn't pregnant. The only girl I'm interested in at this time is you."

She didn't say anything. He reached out and put a hand on her arm.

"How about it? I want to talk to you."

She said, "I don't feel like talking to you now, Cletus."

He said, "You've got to. Time's running out for me."

And her face was suddenly tight with anger, as if a dam within her, too, had burst. And she turned on him. She said, "Fuck off, Cletus."

And when he didn't respond immediately, only sat there looking as if he couldn't believe what he had heard, she repeated it. She said, "I mean it. Fuck off!"

She turned away from him, and for a minute or so sat there quietly, not moving, her eyes on her hands in front of her on the table.

Out of the corner of her eyes she saw the glass in front of Cletus fill once more. Raised, and lowered a moment later. Empty. She heard the chair scrape as it was pushed back from the table. As he walked to the door his shoes crunched on fragments of glass. Then the door opened and closed. And he was gone.

Amy's hand came over and covered Kay's. She said, "Forget him, Kay. You stay here with me and everything will be all right."

Kay pulled her hand away. She said, "Fuck off, Amy!" She said, "I'm telling you, just fuck off!"

Chapter 24

Halfway through dialing the phone number, Cletus paused and looked down at Hank. It was Friday night. They had got back only ten minutes ago from dinner at Sandy's Bar and Grill.

"This is your last chance," Cletus said. "You don't have to go through with this if you don't want to."

Hank said, "I want to. Go ahead."

"I want you to be sure," Cletus said. "I want you to think back on the good things about Mrs. Basil's."

"I remember. Go ahead and dial."

"You could say your prayers every night without anyone giving you any criticism. You could wear a tie and your white shirts and keep your toys piled up neat all the time."

Hank said, impatiently, "Dial the number."

"You'd never have to fix your own dinner, and when you got to the first grade you could do your homework every day right after you got home from school."

Hank closed his eyes and waited for the foolishness to end. He even put his hands over his ears.

"No one would ever tell you any lies and you wouldn't hear any swearing around the Basil house the way you do around here, sometimes."

Hank refused to listen. Cletus dialed two more numbers, then when he had the boy's attention again, added another thought. He said, "A boy doesn't have to be raised by his father, you know. His real father. Or his real mother. There are even kids who don't know where their real parents are. And that's all right. Nobody has to feel bad because he's living with a family other than the one he was born into."

Hank tried to put his hands over his ears again, but Cletus stopped him. "Now listen to me. For I'm serious."

He said, "I know a boy who doesn't even know who his real father *is*. And he's growing up to be a beautiful person anyway, because he's loved. And gives love in return. That's the key. Loving." Then, "Do you understand?"

The boy nodded, impatient. And sighed. But Cletus wasn't quite finished. "I've got to be sure you understand this." He said, "The biological fact of being a father—and by biological I mean, well, like the inherited characteristics. But let me put it another way." And after a moment he said, "Everyone is an individual, and what you yourself are is more important than what your mother or father are. The important thing is that you are able to see life clear and true and to be able to deal with it. Understand?"

Hank said, "No. Dial the number."

Cletus said, "Don't be stubborn. You know very well you understand. You're a bright boy and can think as well as I can."

"Dial the number."

Cletus gave up. He said, "All right, you win. But one last question."

He asked the boy, "Would you want to stay with me even if I *weren't* your father?"

Hank said, "Yes." So Cletus dialed the last digit.

As he waited for someone at the other end to answer, he said, "Now don't forget the things I told you. If you botch this job we're in trouble. So just say the things I told you to say. And the way I told you to say them."

Then into the phone, "Mrs. Basil? . . . Yes, hello. This is Cletus Hayworth.

"Fine, thank you. How about you? . . . Good . . . yes . . . I understand . . . I'm glad Mrs. Bok called you."

He said, "No, but a change of plans. I can't bring him

207

out because he and his mother are leaving for California Monday. But at least you can talk to him on the phone. And that's why I'm calling you tonight. . . . Yes, I'm at his house now to make sure he calls you. . . . No . . . I couldn't say."

He said, "Why she's going to California is her business."

He listened patiently for a long time. "That's true," he said. And after a moment, "True. By coincidence I'm leaving Farmington the same day. . . . Yes, that's why things like that are called coincidences."

Another wait, this time less patiently. "I can't do that, Mrs. Basil. It's the mother's right to decide things like that. And her own mother is protecting her by pretending she doesn't know where her daughter is. As you know."

"Well, talk to Jeorge. Let him tell you. . . . No, his mother doesn't want to come to the phone." And he said, "Okay, hang on."

He turned the phone over to Hank, giving him an encouraging pat on the shoulder as he did so.

"Hang up, dammit."

Hank said, "Hello," in a small, thin voice. And then was silent, listening.

Cletus went to the refrigerator for a beer, then back to where Hank was.

"Yes," Hank said. "She's nice . . . yes . . . yes . . . no."

Cletus stood a dozen feet away and watched. There was nothing he could do now to help. Either the boy could carry it off or he couldn't. "Yes, I got my own bedroom. Yes, two dogs. My mother likes dogs. One's white and one's black. And a cat," he added.

Two dogs and a cat? Cletus laughed.

Hank had at first looked tense and scared. Now he seemed more relaxed.

He said, "No, there aren't men around all the time. . . . Sometimes girls are here."

From the side, in a low voice, Cletus said, "Easy, Hank. Don't ruin it."

"Yes, that's right." Hank said. "Baby-sitters."

After a moment, "Yes, she said maybe she'll get married someday."

He said, "Mr. Hayworth? Yes, I see him lots. He's nice."

Cletus said, "Maybe you'd better hang up. Tell her you've got to get to bed."

That suggestion didn't appeal to the boy. He was now enjoying himself too much to stop. He said, "I don't think I ought to say. I guess who she goes to California with is her business."

Cletus said, "You're going to get us in trouble."

"See him in California? I hope so."

Cletus slapped his hand against the side of his head. This was getting to be too much. He said, "Hang up, Hank. That's an order."

Hank didn't hang up. But he changed the subject a bit. He said, "I got lots of new clothes. And a Frisbee."

"And we eat out a lot. Mostly at Burger Heaven."

Cletus moved to where he faced the boy direct. He said, "I'll count three, and then I'll take that phone from you."

"Sometimes at Sandy's Bar and Grill."

"One."

"I would have called you earlier this evening," Hank said, "but a friend of my mother's stopped by on his way to Peoria to work for the telephone company."

"Two." Cletus held up two fingers. And moved to within a few feet of the boy. He said, in a voice that was soft and friendly, but loud enough for Mrs. Basil to hear, "Better hang up, Hank. Your mother wants you to have your bath and get to bed." And he held up three fingers and looked very stern.

Hank looked at his father, and said into the phone.

"I've got to go to bed now. Yes, I'll write . . . yes . . . yes." Then, "Good night."

And he hung up.

Cletus walked into the kitchen, with Hank following. Cletus carried his miner's helmet. He tried it on one last time, then took it off and pitched it into the wastebasket. He looked angry. He said, "That's it. I'm ruining you, and I admit it." He pushed the helmet to the bottom of the bag, buried it beneath a three-day accumulation of garbage and trash.

Hank said, "You aren't ruining me."

Cletus said, "I certainly am. Ruining you. And I didn't realize it until tonight." He said, "You're getting to be a little damn liar."

Hank said, "I didn't do anything."

Cletus slammed both hands against the sides of his head. "Didn't *do* anything! God!" And he said, "Everything you told her was a lie. And don't try to look so damned innocent."

He mimicked the voice of a six-year-old. "I would have called you earlier, but a friend of my mother's stopped by on his way to Peoria to work for the telephone company."

He swore a few more times, went to where the can of beer was, shook it, saw it was empty, tossed it on top of the trash, and got a fresh can from the refrigerator.

Hank looked into the wastebasket. "You really going to throw your helmet away?"

Cletus said, "Of course. It's not good for you, having your father wearing a miner's helmet around the house."

For a half minute or so, he paced slowly up and down the kitchen. Thinking. Then, he said, "I've probably already ruined you, I suppose. But, by God, from now on things are going to be different around here."

He listed the ways in which things were going to be different. Included in the list was "From now on there is going to be more maturity around this place, as well as more honesty. No more wearing helmets. I've got to start acting like a college-educated man with responsibilities."

And for Hank, "And you're going back to using your real name. Jeorge. Spelled with a J. Because that's your real name. And no lying of any kind from you."

He said, "And next week we're going to pile into that Volkswagen and head for San Francisco."

He looked down at Jeorge. He was softening a little now. He said, "Right?"

Jeorge said, "Right."

Cletus said, "Good." And took time to have a sip of his beer.

He said, "You want to come along?" He was back to smiling again.

"Sure."

Cletus raised his can of beer in salute to that good decision.

"Great." He said, "I'm glad you want to come along. I'd be lost without you.

"So get into your pajamas," he said, "and let's get your prayers over with."

Before Jeorge said good-night, he asked once again, "Are you *really* going to throw your helmet away?" And Cletus said yes. "I've already done so. You saw me do it."

Jeorge found that hard to believe. "You going to get it back out again?"

Cletus said, "No . I told you that. Never."

He had it back on again before the night was over.

Chapter 25

Mrs. Gogle called. She had forgotten whether she was supposed to baby-sit or not. He'd said earlier in the week he'd probably be going out.

He told her he'd changed his plans. He would be staying in. Thanks, though, for calling.

But that started him thinking. Friday night. He wondered who would be at Sandy's. And he almost called her back to say he had changed his mind.

He and Hank had had their last talk for the night. A good talk, as usual, but now he felt like talking to someone older than six, and he tossed aside the book he had started. In his mind he ran down the list of girls he'd have called two months ago. And there wasn't one on the whole list who could have taken his mind off the girl who a little more than twenty-four hours ago had told him to fuck off.

So he called that girl.

Amy answered. She didn't sound very happy herself. She sounded as if she'd been crying.

Kay was gone, she said. She was going to meet someone who was going to give her a ride as far as Cincinnati, Ohio.

Had she left an address where she could be reached? And Amy said she hadn't. Just said that she was headed west. Or southwest. Depending on rides.

So that was that.

He said thanks. And let's hope she comes back some day. And Amy said she hoped so too. And there wasn't much else they could say to each other. So they said good-bye, and hung up.

Again he thought of calling Mrs. Gogle back. And going to Sandy's, and seeing how drunk he could get. But he put that idea aside as a bit too childish for a man with a six-year-old boy he was responsible for.

He dialed Faith's number, just in case she hadn't left yet for Colorado. But she had. That was what Grandmother Hayworth said. Grandmother Hayworth didn't, of course, simply say that Faith had gone. She started way back at the beginning, telling about this boy Faith had met in college, a boy who was studying geology, and she reviewed all the things that had happened between that point and yesterday afternoon when a friend had driven her to the airport. She told it as if maybe Cletus were an acquaintance from years back who just happened to be passing through town on his way to Evansville, Indiana. To work for the telephone company, probably.

For the first two minutes he watched for an opportunity to break in with some excuse for getting off the phone. Then suddenly he realized how much his grandmother needed this talk. And he didn't interrupt her again except once when he broke in to ask if he could be excused. Someone was at the door. And he got a can of beer from the refrigerator and some cigarettes.

Toward the end he told her of a girl he'd known years ago who'd left Farmington to marry a man in Colorado, and now she came back every summer with her children and spent two weeks—sometimes a month—with her family.

She asked him about his plans and he told her he was going west and would maybe buy a mink farm. She thought that was a good idea. She said she hoped he'd be happy. He said he hoped she would be, too.

So that was a nice thing he'd done, and he felt good about it.

213

As a result of doing that nice thing, of listening patiently for over a half hour to a lonely old lady who needed someone to talk to, a nice thing happened to Cletus. He got to see Kay again.

As she said, if she could have gotten him on the phone, she wouldn't have had to stop by.

Cletus was standing by the refrigerator, the door open, ready to reach in for his fourth beer of the evening, when she walked in. She just knocked and walked in.

She was dressed in dungarees and a blue work shirt. Sandals. Hair tied in back. She looked as if she were in a hurry. And nothing at all about her expression implied that she had come to throw herself into his arms.

He closed the refrigerator door, but made no move in her direction.

"Hi! I didn't expect to see you again."

She said, "I stopped by for only a minute. Just to ask you a question. Got someone waiting for me outside."

"Where you headed?"

"West." She wasn't frowning, but neither was she smiling. "Just curious about something."

He said, "You hitching? This time of night?"

She said, "I got a ride." She motioned with her head in the general direction of the parking lot. "Edith Shugrie's father's waiting for me outside. He's going as far as Cincinnati. To bring his mother here from a nursing home, or something."

"Why tonight?"

"He has to be there by tomorrow afternoon."

"Oh." He asked, "Have a drink before you go?"

She shook her head. "The reason I stopped by is that I heard from someone that you were offering a reward to anyone who could tell you how to find Mary Kalinski."

That got a quick response. The very last thing he wanted now was for anyone to tell him how to find Mary Kalinski. He said, quickly, "Too late. It's called off. The person offering the reward has changed his mind."

He'd made his decision and was going to stick to it. He wasn't going to send Hank to live with a prostitute with a drunken husband.

She said, "I'm not interested in your dumb reward. But I came here to find out if you really want to know about Mary Kalinski. And why." And the look on her face made it clear that if there were any stalling someone was going to get a punch in the mouth. "So tell me."

He laughed. "It was a joke more than anything else. Someone who lived here a long time ago knew a girl named Mary Kalinski. He didn't know her very well, but he liked her. He married someone else, though, and when that went sour he thought it might be fun to see if he could locate this Kalinski woman and see if she was still single."

"What was his name?"

"I don't know. He wasn't someone I knew personally. A friend of my sister's."

"Was he a thin, dark-haired man with glasses? About twenty-four by now, I guess. Went to college somewhere near Boston?"

"No. That wasn't how he was described. He is short and fat. With a harelip. Trained in hotel management at Ohio University." He added, "But he just got married again and that's why he's no longer interested and called off the rewards."

She said, "Okay. Just curious," and she turned toward the door. "I've got to go." But she hesitated. She glanced toward Hank's room. Then back toward Cletus. "I almost forgot. There was another reason I stopped by."

"What was that?"

"I wanted to apologize a little for what I said yesterday."

He didn't say anything.

"Okay, so I'm sorry."

He said, "That's all right, I suppose."

"It wasn't because of what April McCartney said. It was other things."

He said, "I don't know what you mean."

"About your having sex with her while you were pretending to be her social worker."

He said, "Christ!" and some other things that expressed vehemently and succinctly his feelings about anything April McCartney might have said.

"Don't get all upset. No one really believed the girl. Eva knew the girl was making up the story when she talked to April a month ago. She happened to mention it to Amy yesterday morning only because of a similar incident that came up. Amy believed it because she wanted to and told it to me as if it were true. But I checked it out myself this morning and realized it wasn't."

Cletus said, "I wouldn't touch the kid. She wanted me to, but I wouldn't."

"So all right. All right. I just wanted to mention it." She looked again toward Hank's room. "I'm sorry I didn't get here before Hank went to bed. I wanted to say good-bye to him."

Cletus wasn't yet ready to forget what had happened yesterday. "I wanted to talk to you yesterday afternoon. I had a lot of things to say. I didn't see why you had to tell me to fuck off."

She shrugged her shoulders. "It's what I had to do, that's all."

"Why?"

"It's a long story. And I've got to go. I told Mr. Shugrie I'd be only a minute."

"Tell me. I need to know."

She thought a minute. "Well, for one thing, lot of what I've told you about myself isn't true."

That was something he could relate to. "I've told you some things myself that aren't true. That was what I wanted to talk to you about yesterday."

"Some of the things that happened to me weren't good. And some of the things I've done haven't been exactly admirable."

"That's all right. You know that."

216

"I used to be a tough kid. Not very bright, but I could at least take care of myself."

He wanted to walk over and put his arm around her, but the expression on her face didn't indicate that that would be what she'd like. He said, "I always thought you were independent. It was one of the things I liked about you."

"Amy's taken care of me the last few months. Before that was a nice man who loved me and I lived with him." She thought a moment. "Now it's time I took care of myself. Not just take care of myself, but get away from Farmington and try to get things together."

"Like what?"

"Like sorting out the things that happened that were good and bad and seeing where I go from here. And I got a lot of learning to do."

"I love you just the way you are."

That got him a nice smile. "Thanks, Cletus. That's always good to hear."

Cletus knew that three or four days from now, on the coast somewhere, she'd swing confidently out of someone's car, thank him for the ride, throw her pack across her back, and look around to see what was happening. And he'd give everything he had to be the one to see her first.

"Actually, I love you very much." Which got another nice smile, but nothing more. He said, "I wish you'd let me go with you."

She shook her head. "I need to travel alone for a while." She glanced toward the bedroom. "I'm going to miss Hank, though."

He said, "Take Hank with you. And me. A package deal. The two of us. Make pancakes. Change tires. Do comedy routines."

"That would be nice." But she shook her head. "I've got to go, Cletus."

He said, "One of the things that I wanted to tell you yesterday was that I inherited some money."

"Good! I'm happy for you."

He said, "I'd like to share it with you."

She shook her head.

"You wouldn't have to pay it back or anything."

She shook her head again, and moved toward the door. But once more she stopped, and again turned to face him. "I know Mr. Shugrie's in a hurry, but is it all right if I see if Hank is still awake?"

He said, "Listen to this. This is my last offer, and it's a good one." He said, "Hank and me and one hundred and forty thousand dollars. Cash."

She repeated the question. "Is it all right if I see if Hank's awake?"

There was a long silence while they looked at each other. A long moment before he was able to move or speak.

Finally he said, "I don't care," turned and moved into the kitchen. "Wake him up if you want to." He bent over the wastebasket and dug out the helmet.

He heard her call from the doorway to the boy's room, "Hank! You awake?"

The helmet had bacon grease on it. And coffee grounds. Ketchup on the inside leather support.

"You awake?"

He shook out the coffee grounds, most of them. And used a dish towel to wipe at the ketchup and bacon grease. He heard her call the boy's name one more time. And no answer.

He put the helmet on and took a few steps closer to where she was, but he didn't move out of the kitchen.

She was standing by the door. She said, "I'm sorry I don't have more time, Cletus. But I don't." And she shrugged her shoulders. That's life. "Maybe I'll see you again some time. I kind of hope so."

"It's not likely."

And she nodded. True. It's a big world. And she opened the door.

"Good-bye, Cletus."

He stood there, hands in his pockets, helmet on his head, and tried desperately to think of something that would keep her from leaving. He would have been willing to lie, even, if he could have thought of a lie that would serve the purpose. But nothing came to mind, so he said the only thing that was left to say.

"Good-bye, Kay."

She said, "Be happy."

He said, "You, too."

She took one last glance behind her before she closed the door. Just in time to see a very sleepy six-year-old boy come stumbling out of his bedroom, blinking at the lights, rubbing his eyes. Hardly able to hold his head up.

So she got to say good-bye to him after all.

She moved quickly over to where he was, gave him a big hug and a kiss. And apologized for waking him. And she told him what a great person she thought he was and how much she was going to miss him. And that she was sorry to be in such a hurry, but someone was waiting for her.

One last hug, then she held out her hand and took his. "So good-bye, Hank."

He shook her hand and gave her a nice sleepy smile. But remembering the new rules, he said, "My name's not Hank."

She didn't understand. And that's what she said to him. "I don't understand what you mean."

Mr. Shugrie was a small, gentle, shy man in his late forties. Rimless glasses, thin gray hair. He went slowly, hesitantly, up the stairs. He hoped Miss Lindsay wouldn't think he was impatient. Or trying to hurry her. But she had said she would be back out in only a minute and he wanted to make sure she was all right.

The door to the apartment was partly open, but he approached cautiously, knocking upon the door frame before looking in.

He could see immediately that she had not come upon foul play, as he had feared.

But she was acting very strangely. She was holding a small boy in her arms and running in crazy circles around the living room, crying or laughing, hugging the child, doing a wild dance, then hugging the child some more. And in the kitchen, watching, looking as if he didn't understand what was going on, was a tall young man with a mustache, wearing what looked like a miner's helmet.

Mr. Shugrie saw his young passenger, still holding the boy, run into the kitchen and grab the mustached coal miner and kiss him, and the three of them, laughing and shouting, danced twice around the kitchen and then into the living room, and the helmet flew off the man's head and rolled across the room and ended up against Mr. Shugrie's foot.

Out of curiosity, he picked it up. There was bacon grease and ketchup on it. And coffee grounds.

And inside the helmet were the words:

M.S.A. SKULLGARD

TYPE K

MINE SAFETY APPLIANCES CO.

PITTSBURGH, PA. MADE IN U.S.A.

THE BIG BESTSELLERS
ARE AVON BOOKS

The Story
All America
Took To Its Heart

A Woman of Independent Means

A Novel by
Elizabeth
Forsythe
Hailey

THE SPLENDID
NATIONAL BESTSELLER

"Nothing about it is ordinary . . . irresistible."
Los Angeles Times
"Bares the soul of an independent American housewife . . .
a woman to respect . . . a writer to remember."
John Barkham Reviews

AVON $2.50

WIM-7/79